Dedication

So often my imagination darts off into wild directions. Through all the weirdness, my readers put their faith in my ability to create a story out of insanity. Thank you for that. Thank you to everyone who supports me. I have to give special thanks to Susan who supported me with my first unpublished stories, reading them and encouraging me no matter what and to my mother who doesn't like my genre, but who never fails to tell me that she's proud of what I've accomplished. Thank you to Mandy who has commented on every single story I've ever written and my Patreon crew including Beth, Alexis, Emma, Sarah, and Maryam who have supported and inspired me. And then there are the wonderful readers who read early drafts and helped me chase down every error from misplaced commas to bizarre continuity mistakes. Thank you Annie, Elf, Janelle, Tracy, Marnie, Amanda, Jean, Vonn, Anna, Haru, Amelia, Htet Htet, Anna, Maryam and Ellie. I appreciate that you don't let me publicly embarrass myself. I save that for Patreon where you see all my mistakes. And to every person who purchases my titles... thank you. You make it possible for me to live in these worlds of my imagination and share them with you.

Chapter One

The belly of the enormous alien ship pushed down through the cloud cover, lightning dancing across its surface of gunmetal gray. Max's stomach twisted in terror, but he focused on his instruments. The invader was as large as a battleship, but Max worried more about the even larger craft NORAD was tracking right behind it. It was large enough to carry an invading army. If Max had to fly his jet up their equivalent of a tail pipe, he would to protect the planet.

Dozens of smaller flyers dropped into the air below the ship. Max could see three different designs, and then all hell broke loose. The ships might have been alien, but Max recognized weapons fire. The tail of Dan-Dan's jet burst into flames, and he punched out, his parachute engaging seconds later.

"Engage bogeys!" Ground One ordered. "Engage! All ships engage!" Fuck. Even the guys on the ground sounded panicked. Despite the fact that none of the jets had opened fire yet, one of the alien flyers exploded. A huge chunk went through Dan-Dan's parachute, and Max watched... helpless... as a pilot he was responsible for sped toward the ground.

Max wanted to tear off his oxygen mask and scream, but he had a job to do. The fear and horror transformed to fury.

He took his F-35 into battle formation and lined up with an alien ship, only to have the damn thing pull impossible Gs as it went straight up into the atmosphere before diving back toward Earth. It was like watching a dolphin doing underwater acrobatics.

7/6/25
8/6/25

EARTH FATHERS ARE WEIRD
Lyn Gala

Earth Fathers are Weird

Copyright © March 2019 by Lyn Gala

All rights reserved. This copy is intended for the original purchaser of this e-book ONLY. No part of this e-book may be reproduced, scanned, or distributed in any printed or electronic form without prior written permission from the author. Please do not participate in or encourage piracy of copyrighted materials in violation of the author's rights. Purchase only authorized editions.

Image/art disclaimer: Licensed material is being used for illustrative purposes only. Any person depicted in the licensed material is a model.

Editor: Sue Laybourn

Cover Artist: Lyn Gala

Published in the United States of America

This e-book is a work of fiction. While reference might be made to actual historical events or existing locations, the names, characters, places and incidents are either the product of the author's imagination or are used fictitiously, and any resemblance to actual persons, living or dead, business establishments, events, or locales is entirely coincidental.

Warning

This e-book contains sexually explicit scenes and adult language and may be considered offensive to some readers. This e-book is for sale to adults ONLY, as defined by the laws of the country in which you made your purchase. Please store your files wisely, where they cannot be accessed by under-aged readers.

"Nose cold. No lock on radar. Negative lock!" Max reported. As the officer in charge, he had to stay cool, so he bit down the more desperate words that clawed up his throat. A new cluster of alien flyers closed on them from two o'clock, and Max barked orders for the wing to adjust formation.

"Ditzy! Bogey at your six! Increase thrust!" Max called. Dee must have punched it because her F-35 pulled away from the cigar-shaped flyer pursuing her. At least for a second, but then the alien accelerated so it passed Ditzy Dee so fast that it made her jet look like a fucking WWI Fokker Eindecker. The alien then shot past Piddle's jet, and he didn't have time to fire.

"Radar is bent. Radar is bent," someone called out. Max pushed his jet toward the deck when his own radar showed one of the larger alien shapes on his six.

"Bells 2, maintain Angels 3."

"I'm punching out!"

"Who has eyes on VJ?"

"Zippy is on the bug; weapon system down."

"Patriot missile inbound. T-minus 45... 44... 43..."

The radio barked out orders and warnings. Max ignored all of them. Below, Earth was a patchwork quilt of fields and Iowa farms. A damaged jet spun toward the ground, crashing in a fiery explosion that sent black smoke into the air. Max didn't even know whose jet that had been, or whether the pilot had punched out safely. Worse, Max hated himself because his first thought was gratitude that his own family lived far enough away that the fire couldn't touch his parents or his little brother.

Max pulled the nose of his F-35 up and the g-forces pushed him toward losing consciousness. At this point, part of him wished he could. Then he wouldn't have to see his world invaded by ships he couldn't hope to fight. He levelled out. Since his computer couldn't lock onto the enemy, Max broke every regulation by opening fire manually.

He must have hit his mark because the alien ship faltered.

"Bells, bogeys closing on you. Firewall that bitch."

Max's heart jumped at the warning and he opened the throttle. His on-board computer warned him as a half dozen ships moved on his position. For a half second, Max froze. He'd never done that, but his brain couldn't decide between punching out or trying to take a few of the enemy with him. He thought of Daniels and the way the aliens had taken out his parachute. If Max was going to die, he didn't want his life to end like that. Not like that.

Ignoring every warning light on his board, Max turned his jet toward the enemy.

He woke on his back in the center of a small room. His body ached, and the sound of that last explosion still echoed in his head. He scrambled to his feet and reached for his radio. And found it gone. Everything was gone. Someone had pulled off his flight suit, and Max was insanely grateful that he'd put it on over his uniform when the alarms had gone off. He couldn't handle captured *and* naked.

Fear made Max's mouth dry, but he called out, "Hello?" The walls deadened the sound. When Max touched the wall, it was smooth, warm metal. The ceiling was covered in what might have been alien pipes or intestines or electrical conduits. He had no way to judge.

An archway appeared on one wall a half second before the crack of light turned into a full door that slid away. Max slipped into a fighting stance. His heart beat against his ribs and the edges of his vision turned gray. Then the alien appeared.

It was short—four and a half to five feet—and the violet mouth reminded Max of his Great Aunt Velma's crazy lipstick. However, the alien's wide face was ringed with the same color, with stripes of purple pointed at her broad nose, and her nostrils were set wider than the corners of her lips.

Max breathed heavily. He braced himself for anything from vivisection to questioning, but instead the alien opened her mouth and wailed. The sound was like an opera singer mimicking fingernails down a chalkboard. Max cringed as shivers ran up his spine.

"Ahh. Okay, I didn't understand that, assuming you were trying to say something to me." Max's chest hurt. He wasn't sure if that was from pulling too many Gs or if he was on the verge of a fear-induced heart attack.

She wailed again, and the sound was so bad it made Max's mouth water, and he had no idea what the hell would cause that. Apparently frustrated with his inability to communicate, she grabbed his arm and jerked him forward so fast that he didn't have time to defend himself or counterattack. He stumbled after her, struggling to keep his feet under him to avoid getting dragged. The ship reminded Max more of a submarine than any aircraft carrier he'd been on. The corridors were narrow with heavy doors separating the sections. If they were in space, that probably made sense.

"That's my planet down there. What are you people doing?"

She dragged him through a door into a corridor with deep bronzy-red walls. Max stopped. Every six or seven feet, a tiny alcove created enough space for one... individual. Many of them were humanoid, but far too many had tentacles or lacked heads. Or both.

"Fuck," he whispered. Next to insectoids, tentacles were on his list of worst nightmares. He hadn't even been amused when one of his boyfriends had wanted to play with a tentacle-shaped dildo.

The short female stopped near an alcove and wailed. A second later, another humanoid appeared. This one was taller and more bulky. The alien's upper lip was huge compared to the lower one, making it look like the victim of a bee sting attack. The alien turned his head, and a half dozen nostrils went up the bridge of something vaguely nose-like. He wailed at the alien holding Max hostage, and she wailed back.

Max said, "I want to go back to my people." He wanted that, but he wasn't sure anyone cared. "Who are you people?" Max demanded. The pair holding him hostage, and probably discussing his painful death, were joined by a third alien. It was shaped like a pith helmet with a curtain of tentacles hanging below. Max shivered in horror.

The lavender alien shrieked, and the helmet wrapped a tentacle around Max's leg. Terror made Max jerk back, but the tentacle held firm. When Max lost his balance, he tried to recover by grabbing lavender alien. That was a mistake. The boss alien shoved Max, and he fell to the ground hard enough to lose his breath. Luckily the floor was the consistency of a wrestling mat, so he didn't injure anything beyond his dignity. He used his new freedom to scuttle toward the door.

Alien bogey one wailed, and Max got his feet under him. He threw himself toward the exit when tentacles wrapped around his knees. Max punched and kicked in every direction. Aliens chittered and bellowed and sang and wailed, using every note on the piano. Tentacles caught Max's wrists, and soon Max could only thrash as the helmet-tentacle alien sat on him. Max might have bitten the nearest tentacle except he did not want *that* in his mouth and he wanted to retain a grain of dignity. He was a military officer. They couldn't strip him of that honor or that responsibility.

A tentacle punched the air next to Max's head, and he flinched away. The tip of the tentacle unfurled to reveal a crystal. A hologram of a tiny television set appeared above the bluish stone. The tiny screen showed television broadcasts. The image switched from one station to another every few seconds, but they were all talking about the same thing—the repelled invasion.

Repelled.

Max's muscles turned watery, and he stopped struggling. Earth was safe. They had repelled the alien invaders. Except Max knew that wasn't true. He'd been in the air, and nothing Earth owned had touched the alien fighters. But in the end, Max didn't care as long as the planet was safe.

After all, his unit had given him the call name Bells after Mr. Belvedere. They'd hoped to insult him by calling him a servant, but Max had always focused on the service part of military service. If his planet was safe, he could handle whatever aliens could dish out until his body failed.

Chapter Two

The pith-helmet, tentacle alien Max had named Spaceballs led Max down a mundane ramp and onto an alien world. In the distance, a city was partially obscured by a greenish, grayish haze that might have been pollution or a poisonous atmosphere that would kill Max. During his days on the ship, he'd discovered that the alien computers had absorbed very little English, so his ability to ask about anything that mattered was extremely limited.

Spaceballs patted the ground with a tentacle. "Here. Here. You seek others here."

Max walked the aisle of the bustling port. George Lucas did not have an imagination this vivid. Aliens of all sizes hurried past one another. Stacks of cartons rolled through the crowd on automated sleds that buzzed in high tones when some tentacle monster stopped too long in front of it. And then the alien in question would wave half its tentacles in the air while the other half carried it clear of the freight's path.

Tentacles, tentacles everywhere.

Okay, that wasn't fair. Only most of the aliens had tentacles. The others had some combination of more leg-like limbs. And several individuals were the same species as the first alien Max had seen. They had a center tentacle that undulated like a snail's underside with two narrow legs on either side. One ran past, her two outer legs lifting the body and flinging it forward to land on the center leg, over and over. Max was developing a killer headache. Maybe the atmosphere was poison and he could look forward to an agonizing death.

"Here, where? Where do I go?" Max asked. In the Air Force, he'd resented how the military dictated every aspect of his life, but right now, he would appreciate a few rules.

"Here. Here." Spaceballs tapped the ground again. The translation computer was particularly fucked today... or Spaceballs hated him. Either was possible.

"Where do I go?" Max illustrated by pointing first in one direction and then the other.

"Here." Spaceballs turned and fled back up the ramp. Max tried to grab him, but the helmet-like top half was too smooth, and his tentacles moved him far too fast for Max to keep up, especially with his stomach churning. He still wasn't sure if that was a symptom of stress or a sign that alien food was killing him, and he was reaching a point where he didn't care. Totally fucked was total and fucked, and whether the level of fuckedness was multiplied by two or ten didn't matter.

The ship door closed behind Spaceballs, and Max was left alone. With nothing better to do, he started wandering toward the city. On Earth, most of the cities he'd seen had a central island of high rises with a wide ring of smaller buildings. However, this city filled the skyline with towers of all shapes and angles. Several grew larger at the top, which seemed like a rather unstable shape for a tower, but Max had to assume aliens understood their own architecture better than he did. To his human eye, it made the city look wrong.

"Human."

Max turned and a ten foot tall alien stood in front of him. "Human. Question." The words came from the translator bracelet on the thing's wrist, but the actual voice came from gill-like slats on the sides of its huge, muscular neck. And it was humanish with two legs and two long arms that hung down past the knees. Of course the arm had a short upper half with an oversized forearm that ended in a four-fingered hand. Or a two-fingered two-thumbed hand. The alien had enough humanlike features that it was more disturbing than tentacle monsters.

"Yes. I'm human." Max studied the triangular underside of the alien's chin, but then the neck sort of folded like a snake bending into an s-shape, and two oversized eyes gazed right into Max's. Max's stomach nearly revolted. The shape of the neck looked too much like it had been broken.

"Designation Heetayu," it said. Given that the translator didn't alter the sound, Max assumed that was either a name or a title, but he was grateful that at least some of the aliens could communicate without screeching.

Max smiled. "Nice to meet you Heetayu. I am..." Giving his full name and rank would probably confuse the alien since Max couldn't explain what the different parts meant. "I'm Max," he offered.

"Mass." The head raised back up. "Come." He strode off.

Max hesitated, but in the end, he didn't have any other resources, so followed Heetayu. They threaded through the crowd. Max tried hard to avoid touching any of the aliens. The occasional alien was terrifyingly large, and a few had bright colors that, on Earth, would suggest the species was poisonous.

None of them paid attention to Max. Either they had seen humans before, or the variety of life forms was so great that no one cared about one more. Max assumed it was the second. It was that or the government had been keeping one hell of a secret. While Max didn't put it past the military to do exactly that in the name of national security, he had to assume that the alien dogfight over middle-America would have caused far less panic if anyone in the chain of command had had a clue.

The alien stepped over a low rail and headed for a mint-colored wall. The wall had a whole series of alcoves, some narrow and others wide, and set into each niche was a computer panel. Heetayu chose a wide alcove and stepped into the shade before turning toward Max.

"This looks interesting," Max said.

Heetayu touched a trident symbol at the side of the panel. Then he said, "Designation interface." It lit up with hundreds of lines and individual displays and alien text. In the upper center, it had a red light that reminded Max uncomfortably of Hal 9000. Hopefully, that was coincidence and not evidence that Stanley Kubrick was trying to warn the human race about the unreliable nature of alien computer systems.

"Interface with what?" Max asked.

"Interface," Heetayu said. "Translator matrix limits."

"Yeah, I'm not impressed with the translation matrix." Max stepped up to the interface. It made the cockpit of his F-35 look like a child's toy. "What do I touch?"

Heetayu then touched dozens of buttons all at once, his eight fingers dancing over the controls. Max had no hope of following the commands he used, but a long tone sounded and then Heetayu reached into a recessed niche and pulled out a translator cuff like the aliens on the ship had worn. He held it out.

"Thanks." Max took the thin metal and looked at it. Before he could do anything, Heetayu took it back and pressed it to Max's wrist. The metal adapted to Max's arm and Heetayu trilled.

"Touch," he said, tapping a two inch glass square.

Max tugged at the translator cuff a second before he laid his fingers on the glass. A new set of lights flashed, and then Heetayu did his finger dance over the controls again. If this was supposed to be some sort of explanation, this guy sucked at his job. But after a second, Heetayu pulled Max's hand away from the glass and then repeated his request.

"Touch."

Max touched it, and this time, the computer made a humming sound. It then squealed. Max flinched, and the second he broke contact, the interface went silent and dark.

Heetayu twitched and the single line of hairs down the back of his head and neck shimmied. "Touch," he said again.

Max felt a need to defend himself. "I was startled." He stepped up and touched the glass again. Once again the computer interface hummed and then squealed. This time Max noticed that the flaps on the front of Heetayu's neck closed. "You don't like the sound either," he guessed. Most animals had some sort of flap or protection over their ears, so it made sense that Heetayu was closing his ears, especially since his own language used the same lower tones as humans. "Does this thing even know English?"

The panel projected a stilted but understandable voice. "Interface updated. Query: Current language. Designation English confirm."

Max had to do a little mental translating to make sense of that. "Yes. Current language is English."

"English. Confirmed. What I assist you?"

Max looked at Heetayu. Since he had two front-facing eyes, Max could tell that the alien was watching him; however, he didn't offer any suggestions. Max only needed one kind of assistance. "I need to find transportation back to my planet."

"Which planet claim you as yours?" The computer asked.

"My planet means the planet where I was born. I don't own it."

"No smart. Logic." Heetayu's quiet voice might have been an admonition for Max to be more logical or it could have been sympathy for the frustration of dealing with a computer. Who knew. However, Max took a deep breath and tried to focus on achieving his goal. "Do you know the ship I came in on?"

"First noted coming from the...." The name of the ship translated as a child's scream. "... fought the Nish illegals... law ... an inhabited planet exterior... trading network."

Max could have cried. Heetayu had understood some part of Max's request, and he had explained why the aliens had come to Earth. Maybe. Max assumed that broken sentence implied that the ship that had taken Max captive had been chasing criminals called Nish. Either that or Max had been on a ship with the Nish. None of that mattered; finding Earth did. "Do you have the location of that planet where they were fighting?"

There was a moment of hesitation, and Max's heart stopped. If he couldn't tell anyone where Earth was, he couldn't find his way home.

After a pause, the computer offered: "Planet..." before ending with a squeal.

"Planet Earth," Max corrected it.

"Updating database—local designation Earth. Transportation queried." The computer paused. "Three ships responding..." More wails.

Max was getting tired of the screeching. "I don't understand the last part of that."

Heetayu pointed at a dark square. "Touch."

Max suspected Heetayu was either a tourist guide or a social worker. He touched where directed and alien symbols appeared. "I can't read that," Max said.

"Touch." Heetayu pointed to a symbol in the lower left corner. The text shimmered and then English words appeared. *Flyer* was followed by a set of alien figures. *Erogingingin* was followed by another. Then three lines listed *Uber* with figures following. Max assumed that the aliens had assumed *uber* was the generic English term for taxi service. That was a lawsuit waiting to happen.

"I don't understand local currency," Max said.

Heetayu lowered his head again. "Currency. Question."

"That's what I'm asking. Currency. Question." Max knew that wasn't helpful, but he had passed the limits of human frustration and was now exceeding the number of problems a saint could handle without losing his mind. "How do I pay for these ships? How much are they charging? Currency. Economics. Money. How do I get and use money?"

Heetayu touched a number of buttons on the interface and then pointed at the glass square again. "Touch."

"This is getting old," Max muttered, but he did as ordered.

"Request currency," Heetayu told him.

Max was fairly sure that any economic system that worked would be more complex than simply requesting money, but he gave it a try. "Request currency."

The computer made a long screeching noise, and Max touched the dark screen before his alien helper could prompt him. Three lines showed up. "What are those?" Max asked. None of the titles were translating into English and the numbers were still indecipherable.

Heetayu's finger hovered over the first line. "Language. Improve translation matrix. English."

"Yeah, your matrix needs some work," Max agreed softly. He wasn't sure he was the man to do the work to improve it. He'd nearly lost his Air Force scholarship over his Spanish grades, and he usually guessed on when to use who versus whom. His English teacher had tried to explain, but Max found it far more complicated than calculus or disassembling an M16. However, if he had to play English teacher to buy a ticket home, he'd grit his teeth and do it. "How much would that pay?"

Heetayu's answer didn't translate, leaving Max to rub his temples as his headache intensified. "Let's try this another way. At that rate, how many years would I have to work to pay for a ticket?" Max wasn't sure that would translate either. After all, he didn't have the vocabulary to ask about food costs or housing. However, it would give him a rough idea of the local economy.

Heetayu reached across Max and typed in a number of commands before answering. "Three hundred and seven Earth years."

Max gritted his teeth and fought back an urge to punch someone. The unfairness of the whole situation pressed against him like a hundred needles stabbing his soul, but there was no one to hit. No one to scream at. Now if Max could get his hands on the captain of the fucking ship that had taken him away from Earth and refused to return him... well, he would happily spend a few hours trying to find vital organs with a dull knife. A sharp one would be too quick and merciful. He took a deep breath.

"I won't live that long, so what are the other options?"

Heetayu lowered his head slowly. "One options pay ticket in three and almost one years."

Max assumed that meant almost four years. Fuck. However, in the grand scheme, that was better than dying of old age on an alien planet. "What do I have to do?"

"Translation matrix failure."

Max closed his eyes and counted to ten. Heroes in movies never had language problems. Alien abduction was not living up to the hype, but hey, at least he had avoided the alien probes. That was a small blessing.

"In return for compensation, what action will I need to take? Will I help improve translation matrix?" Max knew he wouldn't be, but hopefully that would help clarify the question.

Heetayu raised his head again. "Raise young."

"A nanny? Someone wants to hire me as a nanny? Or, someone put out a job that anyone could answer. I could get there and they wouldn't want me." If Max was honest with himself, he wasn't any better with kids than he was with English grammar. Every time he was around his little brother, Max managed to disappoint him or piss him off.

Heetayu touched Max's shoulder. "Jobs only for individual touches..." He pointed to the glass square. "Mass have compensation."

Max frowned. That sounded weird for more reasons than the questionable grammar. "Why would someone hire me to take care of their children?"

Heetayu's head lowered. "Compensation giver. Unpopular. Loud."

A bad boss. Well fuck. Of course Max would travel to another planet and find the alien version of Colonel Wilks from flight school. The man was an asshole, and apparently so was this alien. However, Max had sucked it up to get his papers to fly jets, and to get home, he'd endure a whole lot more than loud. However, he couldn't walk into a job blind. He turned to face Heetayu, hoping that the alien would understand the seriousness of his next words. "I take compensation. Soon after, I regret it. How do I leave?"

Heetayu lowered his head so they were eye to alien eye. "Translation matrix failure."

Max sighed. "I hate that phrase. Okay, question. How do I leave if this compensation giver is too unpopular or too loud?"

"Leave ship. Find console." Heetayu pushed his face toward Max. "Offspring hurt."

Max snorted. He sucked as a babysitter, so he doubted the kids would get close enough to him to suffer any emotional damage if he left. However, maybe alien kids were clingier. "I'll try to avoid hurting offspring. How easy is it to find console?"

"Translation—"

"Matrix failure," Max finished for him. He was grateful he didn't have a sidearm because he was feeling the need to shoot someone. "How many consoles are there?" He looked at Heetayu, but the alien just looked back at him. Max tried again. "Question. Number of consoles?"

Heetayu blinked. "Many."

Right. While vague, that did imply that Max would be able to find help if he wanted to leave the job. Max had signed up for the military despite an equally profound lack of information. Of course back then, Max had been young and stupid and desperate for an ROTC scholarship to pay for college. Now he was middle-aged and stupid, and desperate for a ticket home. Funny. Life hadn't changed as much as Max had assumed. "Let's go talk to this giver of compensation who needs a nanny," Max said with false cheerfulness. If his life was turning to shit, at least he could smile. It always creeped people out.

Heetayu lifted his head back up without reacting to Max's expression.

Unfortunately there was a lack of actual people in Max's life right now.

Chapter Three

Heetayu led Max through a series of ever-smaller lanes. If Max had to guess, he would say they were leaving the official government and military landing sites, passing through the major commercial ones, and heading toward the sort of area where crime would lurk at the edges of society.

Of course, that was assuming this world had criminals who thought as humans did. Max decided that was a safe assumption because this area did not have as many resources allotted to it in terms of computer interfaces and lighting. And fewer aliens walked the lanes. Those who did were larger. The two- and three-foot tall aliens had vanished. Heetayu walked toward a number of enormous ships that squatted at the edge of the yard. Hopefully the aliens inside wouldn't be too big because Max did not want to deal with two-year olds that outweighed him.

"Giver of compensation here," Heetayu said.

Max started second-guessing himself. "Question. Describe giver of compensation," he asked.

"Loud." Heetayu stopped there, so either he was a particularly polite alien or the translation matrix was not up to the job. Max wondered if the aliens had a communication system set up that would allow him to do the translation matrix work as a side hustle. If he had to survive four years of bad translations, he would shoot someone. That made fixing the translation matrix was a mission-critical priority. He wasn't sure what alien jail looked like, but he knew he sure as hell didn't want to find out.

Of course shooting someone required him finding a weapon, but he was resourceful. If MacGyver could make a harpoon gun out of a telescope and mothballs, he could improvise something.

Heetayu touched a short pedestal and the top glowed amber. After several seconds, a hologram of alien letters appeared above the plinth. Heetayu spoke quickly, but the translator only caught a few words. Compensation. Nanny. Human. The hologram vanished, and then Max and Heetayu were left standing outside the closed ship. Since Heetayu didn't seem interested in leaving, Max assumed that meant the employer was coming out to meet them.

"I want to thank you for helping me," Max told his alien tour guide/social worker.

The alien's head came down again. "Translation matrix failure."

Max rolled his eyes. "Of course it did." Since he couldn't communicate anything important, he fell silent—a condition antithetical to him. He might talk slow, but he rarely stopped. Even alone, he kept up a nice monologue, but talking to someone who couldn't understand felt a touch awkward.

The ship gave a *thunk* and the door rose. The alien who appeared fell into the tentacles camp. He had a minty green skin that seemed to be the fashionable color among all the best aliens, but as he glided, he flashed the rusty-red undersides of his tentacles, and the tiny fingers where an Earth octopus would have suckers. A few of the tentacles had red bands near the tips that reminded Max a little of a copperhead. Hopefully the vivid colors didn't mean his new employer was venomous.

He had a thick central tentacle he used for movement, and above a waistline bristling with tentacles, he had a bulbous head. Near where a human's neck would be, he had dozens of eyes, and no two matched. It was as if Jackson Pollock or Dali had painted eyes on an octopus. Max wasn't sure which of the freaky eyes he should look at.

When the alien stopped, it blasted the air with a noise that crossed a whale song with an air horn. Loud. Yeah, that made a lot more sense now. At least the guy didn't use the high tones most of the other aliens did. Those higher pitches hurt Max's ears more than this guy.

"Query: purpose," the new alien's translator said.

Max glanced over to his buddy, but Heetayu was still. Max spoke. "The computer said you have a job." He had no idea if that idea communicated correctly, but the various tentacles all stilled.

"Query: Care for offspring."

"Query: Currency," Max returned. Maybe that was a social faux paus, because both aliens went silent for a few seconds.

Heetayu touched his translator wristband and the new alien retrieved a translator from his weird, floppy tool hat. The two aliens tapped on their devices, and Max stood between them feeling perfectly useless. Normally that brought out his sarcasm, but since this was the only job available for decent pay, he was determined to keep his mouth shut. Eventually Heetayu touched Max's shoulder. "Mass Human. Currency. Agreed."

"How do I access currency?" Max asked. Heetayu blinked at him. Great. Heetayu didn't understand. Okay, he could take this one step at a time. He needed to earn money before he could access it. He turned to the new alien.

"Designation Max," he said.

The new alien said, "Designation" and then made an obnoxiously loud burping sound.

"Yeah. I can't make that noise. Do you mind if I designate you Rick?" Max asked. Hopefully he wasn't jinxing himself because he didn't plan on playing Morty to any narcissists.

"Designation Max," the new alien said. Given the whale song nature of the language, Max was pleasantly surprised to get a recognizable version of his name.

"Designation Max. Yes. Designation...." Max hesitated, gathered his breath, and belched as loud as he could. His sound came out nothing like the alien's, and his mother would have been horrified at Max's bad manners. "Query. Designation Rick?"

The tentacles all pulled back toward the center leg. "Designation Rick," the alien agreed. "Firewalled." He turned and undulated quickly up the ramp. The military term caught Max by surprise. No doubt the aliens had heard any number of pilots calling out that they had their jets firewalled and they still couldn't keep up with the invaders, but the aliens on the last ship hadn't misused the term so badly. Max wondered how many of the men and women he knew were dead now, and how many had gotten back to the ground safely.

Dee always pushed her damn jet too hard, even in training. She wouldn't have bailed out, not unless she found a way to kamikaze right into the enemy. Zip and Piddle were solid pilots, but neither felt their birds the way truly great pilots did. Would they have known when to get out? The emotion caught Max unprepared.

Heetayu touched Max's shoulder. He was definitely more of a social worker.

Max smiled. "I'm good. I guess I'd better firewall my legs, huh?" he said, mangling the term. He patted Heetayu's thick forearm in thanks before he hurried after Rick.

The ship inside was much narrower than the military ship that had picked Max up. With his tentacles spread out, Rick took up the entire corridor. "Query. Human feel offspring not human." Without waiting for an answer, Rick headed deeper into his ship.

Max followed. As the exterior hatch closed, an unfamiliar claustrophobia gripped him, but Max focused on the task at hand, pushing his fears aside. "I think you're asking me if my species likes the young of other species. The answer is yes. I love dog offspring. I like cat and horse and cow offspring." Max tried to remember if he'd been around other babies. He'd had fish growing up, but considering how many of those had died, he should probably avoid mentioning that.

"Query. Dogs."

"Another species. I have raised two dogs. I raised a cow once." Considering that had been for 4-H, Max planned to avoid any discussion of what had happened to it.

Rick stopped at the junction of two corridors and turned in a circle. Max should have chosen a better name because he was getting a brain cramp thinking of this tentacle creature as "Rick."

"Query. Military."

Max stared, not sure what Rick was asking. "I need more words." When Rick let the silence continue, Max added, "Translation matrix failure."

Rick rotated the other way. "Human Max military."

"Yes. I'm an Air Force captain. I fly ships," Max agreed. If this was a job interview, he wasn't sure what sort of answer this guy wanted. Maybe he was afraid Max would lose his mind and chop his children into pieces. Who knew what sort of military personnel he knew.

"Query. Fight."

Max needed to minimize the chance he would lose the only high-paying job he had been offered. "I tried to fight Nish. I didn't do well. No good fighting."

Rick stretched upward so several of his largest eyes were on level with Max's. It meant his huge head and weird hat were pressed against the low ceiling. He must not have had an internal skeleton because his head flattened out. "Translation matrix fail."

Max sighed. "I feel like I'm going to hear that phrase a lot. Deep conversations are not in our future."

"Translation matrix fail."

"Yeah. I got that. It's a good thing I can amuse myself. On the bright side, you've never heard any of the *Star Wars* stories, so I can tell that story and you'll think I'm brilliant. At least until I get to the first trilogy, but I'll change it up. My personal theory is that Jar Jar Binks is a Sith. I'll tell you that version."

"Query. Trilogy."

To hell with shooting someone else. Max might shoot himself. "Query. Offspring." Maybe if he met the kids and figured out what he was supposed to do to keep them out of trouble, he could get his mind off his troubles. With any luck, the kids would be too young to speak and then the language barrier wouldn't even matter. Max would need to figure out how to change alien diapers.

Max frowned and studied Rick's body shape. Unlike most aliens, he didn't wear clothes—only a saddle-like hat that carried tools. That was pressed up against the ceiling right now. However, Max had no idea how Rick or his kids would eat or where the diaper would go. Maybe underneath where the central leg tentacle came out of the center mass? Max forced his mind away from alien poop and looked Rick in the eye... well, the eye that was pointed toward Max.

Rick said, "Query. Health."

"Answer. Healthy."

Rick slid a few inches closer. "Query. Health."

"You want to check my health, don't you? Oh, there are so many *X-Files* episodes I'm flashing back to right now. I truly regret my addiction to television. Deeply regret." Max knew he was being stupid, but his heart rate was still doing a jittery dance.

Rick said in a voice loud enough that it would have rattled windows if any had been around, "Query. Health. Query. Offspring." He followed this with a huge blast of untranslated bugle sounds. That was cursing. Weird, but cursing sounded like cursing in every language, apparently even alien ones.

Max nodded. "Yeah, you're a nervous father. I get it. You don't want me to give the kiddos smallpox. That's reasonable."

One of Rick's large tentacles shot out and wrapped around Max's wrist. "Translation matrix fubar!" he shouted, and Max might have agreed—enthusiastically agreed, even—only he had to focus on keeping his feet under him as Rick dragged him through a maze of corridors. For a creature with one tentacle leg, Rick was graceful and fast.

"Hey! Wait. Slow down," Max gasped out when they stopped in some sort of transport. His stomach lurched when the diagonal movement didn't match any direction he had anticipated. Rick braced his tentacles against the transport walls, and the space was so small that Max ended up pinned into a corner by two of them. The transport jerked to a halt and the door slid up.

"Can we talk—?" Max ended with a squawk when Rick rushed him down another claustrophobic corridor. They stopped next to a door, and Rick let Max go. For a half second, Max contemplated running, but first, he needed the job. Second, he didn't know how to get out, and third, he sympathized with Rick's frustration at their lack of communication. He didn't approve of the grabbing and dragging, but he'd been known to do something similar with his brother when the twerp frustrated him.

Max felt a needle-prick to his heart at the thought of Petey. He'd be at least twenty before Max would be able to get home again. Assuming Max could get home.

"Let's talk. Communicate," Max said hopefully. The door folded in on itself like an accordion, with the folds disappearing into the top of the doorway. Inside was a space just as tight the others he'd seen on this ship, but this one had a tilted table in the middle. Max's imagination went into overdrive.

Rick blurted a huge burped conversation, but the translator only caught three words: confirm, health, and firewalled. Rick's computer translator appeared to have picked up a different set of words than the translators on the first ship, and Max wasn't impressed with how it used them.

"Right. So, I guess this is where we do the whole checkup. You'd better keep your tentacles to yourself." Max eased into the room. Since Rick was ninety percent tentacle and had no other way to use instruments, Max figured he didn't have good odds on that, but a man could hope.

Chapter Four

M ax stood beside the low table and wondered what he was supposed to do. For all the earlier rush, Rick didn't seem interested in hurrying now. He went to one wall and spent significant time sticking his tentacles into various holes and grooves. "My mother always told me I shouldn't stick a finger in a light socket," Max said. "But then Wile E Coyote taught me the exact opposite, so who am I to judge?"

Rick ignored him.

Max wondered if Rick was watching him. The fact he had eyes scattered all the way around his head ranked high on the freaky scale. And given that Max had spent the last several days living on an alien ship—that was saying something. His freak meter had reached terrifying new levels. A hologram rose in the middle of the table—a tiny human figure. The hologram got larger and shifted to display a vascular system. "Query," Rick said.

Max sighed. He preferred it when Rick lost patience and dragged him across the ship. At least then Max wasn't risking death by boredom or frustration. "I'm going to get sick of hearing that word, aren't I?"

Two tentacles twitched. "Query."

Max sighed. "Blood. Vascular system." And that started the most boring four hours of Max's life since he'd taken the SATs in high school. He identified hundreds of words for various parts of the human body. When Rick decided he wanted to check the health of his new nanny, he took that job seriously. Eventually, the digestive system led to discussions of intestines.

Rick zoomed in to show the wall of the intestines, and as the tiny sliver grew to fill the whole hologram, candy-shaped structures wriggled. "Ew." He had been half lying on the desk, but now he took a step back.

"Query."

"Yeah, yeah. Either I've picked up alien parasites or those are bacteria."

Two of Rick's tentacles shook. "Query!" he said louder. Apparently he didn't like ambiguous answers.

His temper fraying, Max shouted back, "Bacteria!"

Rick ran the scan down the intestines, the camera view turning and twisting to show different segments. "Query bacteria."

"Answer. Digestive system," Max said. He had no idea how to reassure Rick that bacteria were normal. Hell, maybe Rick thought the bacteria was the intelligent life form he'd hired and Max was the meat suit it was wearing. Max got an up close and personal view of his colon all the way to the end before Rick shifted to the reproductive system.

At least he didn't obsess over it as much as the bacteria, although Max did spend too much time looking at his own sperm. He was grateful when Rick moved the scan down to his feet. "Check health," Rick said.

"Yeah. I thought that's what we were doing."

Rick slid a few inches closer. "Health offspring." A thinner tentacle darted out and ran up the cuff of Max's uniform shirt.

Max jerked his hand away. "Whoa. Hey. Bad touching."

Rick blasted the air with his weird musical belching and caught Max's shirt. Before Max could free himself from the tiny finger tentacles holding him, another tentacle had pushed his shirt up and over his head. Rick had some real muscle, because he lifted Max onto the table.

"Rude much?" Max asked, but then one tentacle pressed a flat instrument of some sort against Max's cheek while another pulled at his undershirt. "Yeah, yeah. Don't rip it. It's not like I have anything else to change into. As it was, Max needed to figure out washing facilities. On the military ship, those had been marked, so Max only had to look for the symbol shaped like a worm with three horns. So far, none of Rick's doors had any signs. He stripped off his undershirt and put it next to his uniform shirt on the edge of the table. At least Rick had been polite enough to keep it off the floor. The whole time, Rick kept the cool metal instrument against his cheek.

"Query." Rick followed that with another blast of words, these closer to whale song than burping.

"Yeah, I didn't get any of that," Max said, but then a tentacle reached for his waistband. "Okay, so we're going for the full physical. I would normally ask that a nurse sit in for this part." He slid off the table/desk and unbuttoned his pants. When Rick had first started asking about his health, Max had expected the full monty. The existence of the magical scanners had given him a glimmer of hope that he could avoid it. "I suppose I can't blame you. I'd feel guilty if I gave them the measles." He folded the pants and underwear and put them with his shirt and undershirt. "I don't know whether your nudity makes this better or worse."

"Translation matrix failure."

"Yeah, yeah." Max got back onto the table, his bare ass right over where the hologram appeared. He felt like a kid trying to photocopy his butt. Rick pressed the flat metal against Max's thigh.

"Health offspring digestive system."

Max frowned. "I don't think my gut bacteria will hurt your kids." He didn't know if that was true. Neither college nor the Air Force had covered cross-species contamination with aliens. Thinking of home caused an all-too-familiar jolt in Max's gut, so he pushed those memories away. It couldn't afford to get maudlin, especially when he was flirting with depression. It was one thing to sit around with a beer and good-naturedly gripe to his friends about the promotions board being full of shitheads. It was quite another to let himself dwell on all the ways life had kicked him in the teeth.

"Do you ever wear clothes?" Max asked his many-tentacled boss. "I mean, the guys on the other ship had wide belts or skirts and one even had tentacle pants, but you're letting it all hang out. Or it would hang out if I knew what your balls looked like." Max frowned as he considered the various tentacles. They were different shapes, some bulbous and some tapered. One of them might have been Rick's penis, assuming he had one. Rick might have been a girl. Maybe caring for children primarily fell to the parent who gave birth to them.

Rick curled a tentacle around Max's thigh and yanked up fast enough that Max fell and would have slammed the back of his head against the table if another tentacle hadn't caught him. "Warn a guy!" Max shouted.

Rick blasted out something, but the translator only caught "acceptable," "offspring," and "health."

"Yeah, yeah. Sadly, you still have a better bedside manner than my Air Force intake doctor." Max kept up a steady stream of conversation and avoided thinking about the tentacles mapping his skin. "I don't know whether he wanted to weed out the weak or if he took exception to me because I'm gay. Who knows? It's hard to tell who dislikes me and who dislikes my sexual orientation, which is why I try to avoid those conversations. You're a pretty good listener, did you know that?"

A tentacle brushed against Max's cock. "Whoa. That is a little personal."

Despite the fact that Rick had ignored Max's whole monologue, this caught his attention. He said, "Query. Define personal."

"You are touching parts of me that even the military didn't touch. And I thought their physicals were pretty invasive." Max drew out the word pretty.

"Query. Pretty." The translator mimicked Max's pronunciation.

Max gave a braying laugh. "I'm pretty sure you want to define invasive." A tentacle slid between his balls and over his hole. Max yelped and scooted back a few inches, which was how much slack he had before the tentacles drew tight. "Whoa. That. That's invasive." His voice was dangerously high. "That right there is invasive."

Rick stopped. A couple of tentacles pulsed against Max's leg, but everything else grew still. "Query. Compensation. Offspring."

Max drew a breath. Right. If he wanted compensation, Rick needed to check out those scary, scary bacteria. One little anal probe by an alien tentacle was absolutely not more terrifying than flying a jet fighter against alien invaders. Hell, it wasn't even as scary as his ROTC commander. Even his dad trumped tentacles for sheer terror, although he refused to think about family while naked. Nope. Some psychological trauma was not worth it.

"Answer. Compensation," Max said. One tentacle slowly slid up his back. Max took a breath and looked away from the bulbous head hovering near his right shoulder. The tip of a tentacle pushed against Max's ass.

It had been a while since anything had gone up there. Duty had kept Max so busy that he'd barely had time to masturbate in the shower. Hell, he'd gone steady with his right hand so long that it would have gotten jealous if Max had tried playing with a dildo. So the feel of something sliding into him sent unfamiliar shivers through his body.

"Thank God you use slick," Max said.

"Query—"

"Answer!" Max shouted. He couldn't deal with Rick's annoyingness and his tentacles at the same time. Rick made a sound like a long trombone note, and then pushed his tentacle in faster.

"Oh fuck!" Max gasped, and technically he wasn't wrong. That felt like fucking. Too much like fucking. Why the hell had he ever objected to Daniel's tentacle dildo toy? If anything, the porn that Max had read and vowed to never admit to reading had underplayed the sexual prowess of tentacles. Even though Max knew Rick was only interested in checking out gut bacteria, the undulating movement against Max's prostate was driving him past the point of coherent thought. Rick made a fluttering trumpet noise the translator didn't catch at all. Maybe Rick was expressing surprise that his new nanny was a fucking tentacle whore.

Max took a deep breath and tried to calm his racing heart. That didn't help his cock situation, but even the thought of Old Man Wilson with his nose hairs and black acne couldn't counteract the evil brilliance of Rick's tentacle. The damn thing swelled and bulged, and the delicious stretch made Max's ass hunger for more.

"Query. Blood flow increase."

"Oh hell yes." Max gripped the edges of the table and fought an urge to jerk off. He was pretty sure that ejaculating on your boss was bad manners in any galaxy, but if Rick didn't finish soon, that's exactly what would happen.

"Query. Blood flow changes."

That was it. Max was in hell. He was getting the best ass stretch of his life. His ass was full of twitching, swelling tentacle until his brains were leaking, and the damn fucking alien wanted to have a fucking conversation. This was hell. Max's dick threatened to explode, and that would be the perfect shit cherry on life's sundae.

"Query. Blood flow changes," Rick repeated. He also twitched his tentacle. Max's cock leaked pre-cum.

"Answer. Reproductive system." Max held on to the table harder when Rick tugged his tentacle. Whatever he was doing up Max's butt, his tentacle appeared to have gotten stuck, so he gave several tugs. Each time, the pressure increased against Max's prostate, and Max fought the instinct to buck his hips.

Never one to pass up a chance to be annoying, Rick said, "Query. Blood flow changes."

Max gasped, not able to answer immediately as his brain suffered a small white-out. His ass was stuffed so full that he feared he might split in half. Of course if that happened, he would die a happy man. Rick gave another tug, and the pressure edged over into pain. It was enough to anchor Max to reality for a moment. "Answer. You are turning on my reproductive system."

Rick grew still. Eventually he asked, "Query. Human offspring. Now. Soon."

Max laughed. "No offspring. I need woman with a different reproductive system to make offspring. And no offense to the women in my life because I love many of them deeply, but I would cut off my dick before I would put it in a woman." He respected bisexual men, but he was not anywhere near the middle of the scale. If he wanted kids, and he did one day, he would have to find a nice man to settle down with and look into adoption. As hard as it was for a gay couple to get a kid, the system was impossible for a single man.

"Query. Woman."

"Man reproductive system plus woman reproductive system leads to offspring," Max said. "How is this my life now? I feel like I'm trapped in a spaceship with a three year old... oooha." Max's voice rose to a squeal as Rick's tentacle caused a stomach cramp so severe that Max's stomach rippled and contracted. "Fuck. Shit. Fucking shit." Max writhed in pain. "Oh Lord. Too much. Too much."

"Within tolerance health," Rick said calmly, but tentacles began to massage Max's stomach. Those little tentacles on the underside of the big tentacle all worked together to press at the offending muscles until the cramp eased. Unfortunately, Rick seemed to feel that Max's cock was part of his stomach and involved in the whole cramping problem. A tentacle wrapped around Max's dick, teasing him with tiny finger tentacles. When Rick squeezed gently, Max bucked up into him. And wasn't that embarrassing. Max would have stopped if his body hadn't hijacked all higher brain function.

He thrust into Rick's grip, and the friction against his cock combined with the stretch in his ass generated fireworks. Max's whole body went stiff and then jerked twice before he came all over himself and Rick. Creamy flecks landed everywhere... Max's stomach, Rick's tentacles, the table. Max collapsed back and gasped. Option one, he was having a heart attack. Option two, it had been too damn long since his last orgasm. Option three, when shoving things up the ass for fun and pleasure, tentacles worked better than dicks. Max was leaning toward three, although two was also true, and one was a distinct possibility.

Rick's tentacle was now painfully large, but he was slowly pulling his tentacles back. No more of the hard tugging or undulating, just a slow, steady withdrawal. So the guy did know how to be careful.

"Query. Health. Human."

"Oh, I'm fucking great," Max said. "Thank you for asking. You're much more polite than the typical tentacle monster, although honestly I don't have experience with the non-fictional kind." Max knew Rick couldn't understand more than a word or two of that, but he didn't care. He didn't care about much right now. Rick had reduced Max's thoughts to "tentacles good."

"Query. Health." Rick moved closer so his misshapen head floated over Max.

Max blinked up at his alien employer. "Answer. Health great. Good. Awesome. Fabulous."

Two tentacles curled up close to the head of Max's cock while the last of the tentacle inside Max slipped free. "Query." Rick blasted the air, but he touched a milky white drop.

"Answer. Cum. Semen. Sperm. Reproductive fluids. Dick juice. Pearls. I had a boyfriend who called it that last one, and honestly, I don't get it. It's not a solid, and if my semen were made out of pearls, I'm pretty sure it would hurt. Maybe he was trying to tell me he was interested in sounding, but if so, he was way too subtle about it." That had been Max's second real boyfriend, and the first one he'd been willing to touch when the lights were on. Sure, his family and friends were supportive, but Max had still been a little weirded out about touching another guy where someone might see, even if the someone in question was Max.

He assumed heteros were equally weird, given the sort of shit they talked about on daytime television, like that one woman who was in danger of a divorce because she wouldn't let her husband see her without makeup. Max wasn't that bad. Hell, he didn't even own makeup. At least he hadn't since that brief goth phase his sophomore year.

"Query. Health," Rick said.

Max levered himself up and sat on the edge of the table. He was pretty sure he was worrying the boss. "Query. Offspring," Max said. A little change of subject sounded like a good idea.

"Offspring. Health. Proficient." With that, Rick swiveled on his leg and undulated his way out of the examination room.

"You didn't even buy me flowers," Max complained softly. Honestly, though, he was grateful that he wasn't losing the job because his gut bacteria was toxic. Losing this job would suck. Accidentally killing alien children would suck worse.

Chapter Five

With a sigh, Max cracked his back and stood. He was pretty sure the "chair" Rick had found him was an alien torture device. The sloping top and awkward height didn't lend themselves to working on the translation matrix for long periods of time. And like all the "rooms" in the ship, there was barely space for him to stand and take two steps. At least this room was larger than his sleeping quarters. The single-sized fold out bed filled every inch, and he had to lift it to access the washing or toilet. If it weren't for the fact that every surface had stiff padding, he'd feel like he was on a submarine.

And the computer didn't make his life easier. Either the computer thought Max was a brain damaged four-year old or the system was set up to maximize frustration. After identifying twenty different colors as "blue," Max never wanted to see the color again. And he couldn't figure out how the system chose topics. One hour he would be identifying colors, and the next looking at pictures of impossibly complex machines as the computer highlighted certain parts for translations.

Maybe that's why the computer thought he was an idiot.

The door opened, and relief washed through Max. Awkward half-conversations with Rick were infinitely better than working on the computer matrix. "Rick, my buddy, my friend. Save me from the evil computer."

One of Rick's tentacles twitched. Max needed to up his game. On good days he could get three or four of them to curl. "Translation matrix has failed," Rick said. "Define evil."

"Evil. Sadistic. Serving the dark forces. Causing pain. The enjoyment of others' pain. Evil."

"Query. Correlation Darth Vader."

"Exactly," Max said happily. He might have been trapped light years from home with no idea of where home might actually be, but at least he could corrupt an entire new species. Max took his pleasure where he could find it.

"Query. Do does what how Max designate computer to call Darth Vader?"

That had been as clear as crude oil. Max made a mental note to work with the computer on the structure of questions. "Answer. No. I dislike computer now. Darth Vader is evil always."

"Computer dislikes you," Rick said. Either the computer had an artificial intelligence or Rick was developing an attitude. Max liked it. Rick waved his talking-tentacle, the one most likely to twitch or curl when communicating. "Come for health to offspring."

"Query. When will I see offspring?"

Rick's answer was a cacophony of untranslatable notes. So far the computer and Max had found no common ground on time, despite the fact that the computer at the common dock could calculate years. Or maybe it hadn't. Maybe it had been trying to communicate something other than time. Either way, Max sucked at estimating a minute, because this computer kept informing him that his examples failed to match. It would have helped if the military ship hadn't confiscated every piece of technology, including his wrist watch. Until he figured out how to count to sixty-Mississippi accurately, any discussions of time ended in failure.

Apparently they would go pick up the kids when Rick was good and ready. Until then, Max was free to wander the ship and work on translations. "Right. So what are we doing for the health of offspring who are not even on the ship?"

Rick pivoted on his leg tentacle and left the room.

Max muttered, "Okay. Sure. I'd be happy to go with you. Thank you so much for asking." Sarcasm was so much more effective when the other person understood English. In some ways Rick was the best roommate he'd ever had. Rick would not only listen to Max ramble on about something hopelessly geeky, but he asked questions that made it clear he listened and thought about what Max had said.

In other ways, living with him was all kinds of frustrating.

Rick took the passage that would take them to the interior of the ship. So far Max had focused more on the outer corridors. They were larger and allowed Max to run laps. His explorations had revealed that the ship was less a maze and more a spider web of corridors that crossed and re-crossed.

Experienced servicemen and women loved to play head games with newbies lost on various ships and bases. Navigating them were infamously difficult. However, Max dared anyone to compare an airbase to the crazy logic of alien ships.

"Query. Where?" Max asked.

"There," Rick answered.

"I should have seen that coming. You are very Yoda-like. Yoda was Luke Skywalker's teacher. I should probably tell you that Luke is the real hero of the story. I just like Darth Vader's story more."

"Darth Vader evil."

"Yes."

Rick stopped and leaned toward Max. "Query. Evil, preference for."

Max had stuck his foot in his mouth that time. "No. I don't like evil. I find evil interesting to talk about." The last thing he needed was for Rick to decide that Max couldn't be trusted around children. As it was, he kept pressing about Max's time in the military. Maybe he still had Max on a probationary period. If so, he was one seriously overprotective parent of indiscriminate gender.

Rick bugled something untranslatable and then headed down the corridor again. Hopefully Max had passed the test and convinced his boss that he wouldn't turn the children to the dark side. However, Max should probably avoid *Star Wars* discussions in the future.

Maybe *Babylon 5* with its message that evil was more about misunderstanding and selfish manipulations would be more in keeping. Then he could give Rick the impression that he was a conniving manipulator and not a psychopath. That would be so much better. "Or I need to learn to keep my mouth closed," Max said aloud. He had always been a social man and this isolation was driving him a little batty. If he had to police his language, he might have the psychotic break Rick clearly worried about.

A door slid open and Rick glided into a room with a giant pool in the center. "Oh my God. Is that a swimming pool?" It was more likely a radioactive cooling tank, but a man could dream. This was the largest open space he had seen yet. Gently sloping sides went all the way around the room and in the center was a round, larger-than-Olympic sized pool. Quick currents moved out from four pipes that rose from under the water and each had stair-step rocks around it so it created small waterfalls that darted down the uneven surface, randomly changing their chosen path from one second to another.

"Query. Define swim."

That was tricky. If the water was contaminated or radioactive, Max absolutely did not want to give Rick the idea that he wanted to get in. So instead of answering, he asked a question of his own. "Query. Is water safe?"

"Healthy," Rick assured him, and then, as if to prove his point, he walked straight down the slope and into the water. As the water rose over his tentacles, Rick began to wave them in octopus-like ways. Max looked away. Rick's nudity might be normal for him, but every once in a while, Max had pornographic thoughts that made him feel like an ass. After all, Rick had only wanted to do a physical exam, and thanks to Max and his uncontrolled dick, things had gotten awkward.

"Query. Define swim," Rick asked again. The water muted his natural voice so it sounded more musical, but the voice from the translator on his hat sounded the same. Max glanced at his wrist translator. If it died, Max would be more screwed than ever. However, if he took it off, he wouldn't be able to speak to Rick. Max moved to the door, and in a millisecond, Rick was out of the water and standing near him, all his tentacles twitching.

"Answer," Max said. "Swim is to move, to walk, in the water."

Rick's tentacles stilled. "Query. Human preference for swim."

"Answer. It varies. I love to swim. Translator. Leave here. I will swim." Since the floors sloped slightly, Max didn't want to have such an important piece of equipment in the room. He opened the door and set the translator next to the wall in the corridor. Now Rick wouldn't be able to understand anything he said, although Rick's translator would still be able to generate English.

Once the door closed, Max stripped off his clothes. As much as the tiny sink in his quarters sucked for washing clothes, he should've worn them into the water, but then he wouldn't have had anything to put on when he got out. The ship wasn't particularly warm.

Taking the translator off freed Max to speak his mind. "If this were a porn, I know exactly how it would end." He tested the water temperature with his foot. It had a touch of chill, just enough to encourage swimming rather than lazing around on a floaty. Throwing caution and the risk of radioactive contamination to the wind, Max belly flopped into the water and then dove under the surface. The four currents made the water unpredictable. He dove deep before touching the sloping bottom of the pool.

When he broke the surface, he gasped, both because of the need for air and because Rick was inches away, a large eye right in Max's face.

Max flopped backward. "Hey. Warn a guy," he complained before he did a few backstrokes.

"Query. Swim Max currently?" Rick asked.

"Yes," Max said, even though without the translator, he didn't give Rick good odds of understanding. Maybe he had figured out the simpler English words—those Max used often. He flipped around and switched to a breast stroke to cover the distance to the far side. Most rooms on the ship were little more than cubicles with one entrance. Others were central hubs with a dozen exits. This room had two doors. Weird. Max was equally baffled about why aliens would install a swimming pool. Sure, The Doctor had had one, and watching Leela swim had nearly made Max reconsider his sexual orientation. However, fictional aliens didn't have much in common with real ones.

More than that, Max had no idea how one navigated with this much unstable and unsecured weight. If the ship had any gravitational forces pulling at it, the mass of the water would be an absolute nightmare. He had certified on a 135 Stratotanker, and that thing had flown like a fucking tank with wings. But this pool held more water than that old beast had carried fuel. Rick had mad piloting skills or the computer had an autopilot with crazy computing capabilities.

Max dove under the surface again and kicked through the water. The slide of warm tentacles across his leg startled him so much that he lost his air and had to surface fast. Again, Rick was right next to him. "Okay, you have to keep your tentacles to yourself because I am having pornographic flashbacks to my last checkup. Honestly, you could make a killing as a naughty doctor if you ever moved to earth. I know people who would pay a whole lotta money for a little tentacle love."

Max backstroked away from the tentacles floating in the water around Rick's head. "I feel totally guilty about how I reacted to what, for you, was a health exam. I know human doctors are generally unamused when someone comes all over them. Of course, I came on myself as much as you, but that's not the point."

Max wasn't sure what the point was. Rick swam closer, but he was moving slower now.

"You know something is wrong, but you won't ever guess what. I'm caught between humiliation and guilt. You know, I've jerked off a couple of times thinking about your tentacles, and considering you're my boss, that's in the not-good column. I turned a medical exam into a sexual situation when you don't even understand what happened. I'd confess what a shitty human being I am, only I don't think the translation matrix is up to conveying feelings yet. If it were, you probably would have shared your thoughts. Hopefully you're confused and not grossed out by the human spunk you got on your tentacles."

Max turned in the water and swam away. He saw Rick swimming for the edge, his head held up while all his tentacles did the spread and swoosh thing Max had seen in videos of octopuses. He climbed out and headed for the door, and Max switched over to floating. The current dragged him closer to a tiny island with a miniature waterfall. When he drifted close enough, he put his hand out and let warmer water run over his palm.

Rick didn't even let the door close before he returned. He swam closer and raised his tentacle with Max's translator held firmly in his finger tentacles and water running off it.

Max sighed. "I seriously hope that's waterproof." He fastened it around his wrist.

"Query. Human swim, human walk, preference."

Either the translator was improving or Max was getting better at filling in the words Rick didn't use. "Preference walk. Swimming is enjoyment."

Rick gave another whale blast and Max was grateful the water dulled the noise. Rick then added. "Query. Correlation swim and run."

Max laughed. When he'd started running the outer corridors, that had upset Rick to no end. It had taken Max almost an hour to pry all Rick's tentacles off him and explain that humans were healthier and happier if they ran. Rick pretended to understand, but every time Max ran, Rick would show up. Unless Max missed his guess, Rick considered him slightly brain damaged. At least Rick supported his swimming.

"Answer. High correlation swim and run. I enjoy both." Max gasped when tentacles gently brushed his leg. Rick made self-control difficult. Max swam backward to get a little more distance between them.

"Humans are..." Rick ended with a belching sound. Max was pretty sure he didn't want to know what Rick was saying. He gave another set of blasts, this time a mixture of burps and whale song. The translator only sent through "children" and "healthy."

"That's good. Query. Can I see them?" Max swam farther away, but Rick followed. Another brush of tentacle against ankle made Max think such dirty, dirty thoughts. He was lucky the water was cold as a bitch or his cock would've been impossible to control.

"Not visible. See at time to come."

"As paranoid fathers go, you're good. You're good. If you have a daughter, I suspect a shotgun will feature in her future dating life."

"Translation matrix—"

"Failure. Yeah. Shocking." Life hated Max. But if the only way to improve communication was to go back to the damn matrix improvement project, he would have to suck it up. It wasn't like he had anything else to do until Rick decided to go pick up his kids.

Chapter Six

Max floated in the salty pool water and stared at the ceiling. Long curving ribs and a web-work of support cables filled the dome. All the other rooms in the ship were featureless. Bunks, sinks, cabinets, wiring, and structure were all hidden behind padded doors. While practical, it made for boring rooms, even compared to the military bases where Max had been stationed. On the practical side, it would make the ship far safer if they ever lost artificial gravity.

When Max bumped into the water filtration island, he turned and swam slowly toward Rick. He floated with all his arm tentacles spread out like a starfish with his big head bobbing in the middle.

"Why have most of the ships I visited so far had the same gravity?" Max asked. He got the feeling that Rick wanted to talk. Max worked on the translation matrix by himself for hours every day, but the second he started to run laps through the outer corridors, Rick would show up. At first Max assumed Rick was confused. Actually, he still thought Rick was confused. Rick had a habit of watching with the same expression Max had when watching reruns of *Twin Peaks* out of order. In both cases, they knew something important was going on, but it wasn't clear what.

However, Max assumed Rick felt more than simple curiosity. Maybe he was lonely without his kids around, or maybe he was suffering an alien version of divorce or a child custody dispute. He was downright stalkerish when Max came for a swim. Max couldn't do more than a lap or two around the center islands before Rick glided in on his single leg. Rick struck him as a lonely man. Alien. Whatever. Max sometimes wondered if the children were imaginary. Maybe Rick wanted a friend and feared rejection. Even without compensation, Max would happily hang out with Rick. He was fond of Rick and his randomly scattered eyes and his love of any story with Darth Vader.

"Most ships make gravities similar," Rick said. The translator still had a slight awkwardness to it, and some concepts led to entire failures of vocabulary, but overall, Max was quite proud of his work on the translation program. That had been downright understandable.

"Query. Why is that? Have all the different aliens gotten together and decided to use the same gravity?" Max considered that from a pilot's perspective.

Logistically, that would've been safer than navigating wildly unpredictable gravity wells when approaching another ship or station. Having a standard would prevent pilots from having to calculate the forces that gravity would apply to the ship. Otherwise, somebody would do the equivalent of driving through a laundromat's front window. When that happened in Wichita, it was an interesting item on the news. If someone's tentacled Uncle Bob drove his spaceship through a station window, Max was fairly certain that people would die.

"No. All creatures in ships like gravity that they like."

Max righted himself and dog paddled next to Rick's large tentacle. "Are you telling me that all of these different aliens have similar gravity on their home planets?" That didn't make a lot of sense. But then again, Max was quickly discovering that the universe didn't care about his personal opinion of it.

"Yes."

Sometimes those one word answers made Max want to tie Rick's tentacles in a knot. "Clarify. Query. Why would everyone's planet have the same gravity?"

"Many planets are many gravity different."

"Exactly. If everyone has a different gravity on their home planet, then why are all of the ships using similar gravity?"

Rick twirled until he considered Max out of a new cluster of eyes. "Different planets have many gravity different. However. Clarify. Most who travel space have gravity similar."

"Why?"

Rick's tentacles twitched. Max grabbed the edge of one of the water filtration islands and pulled himself half out of the water. Thank God he had taken a job with a patient alien. Even if it caused him tentacle-twitching frustration, Rick would explain a dozen different times if Max asked him to. In his whole life, Max had never been able to talk to someone the way he could to Rick, and that said something sad about Max's love life.

"Planets of large create more gravity." A few details came through only as untranslated belches, but Max understood the bulk of the statement.

"Yes," Max said.

"Big planets have many metals. Elements owning large electron numbers."

As the translator struggled with technical terms, Max realized that he needed to do a little clarification of the periodic table. That said, he did understand what Rick was talking about. Large planets would have more heavy metals and radioactive materials, more nuclear fuel, and basically more raw materials for building a spaceship. If they were playing a world building game, Max would want to start his civilization on a big planet.

"Yes, and with more of those metals, they could reach space. And then they would be here with ships that used heavy gravity. Where are the ships with heavy gravity?" Max asked.

"No. Clarify." Rick paused, and Max could almost see the thought bubbles over Rick's head as he struggled to find a way to explain concepts that were obvious to him, and not-so-obvious to Max. "Big planets mean difficult lifting. Ships fall back to big planets. Those ships are not in space."

"Oh." Max grimaced. Gravity trapped some cultures. "Are there large planets with big civilizations that can't get off?"

"Yes. They trade in information or communication. They send up ships too small for a pilot. Sometimes traders drop materials into gravity well. They do not travel space."

"Okay. That makes sense. That also sort of sucks. My people have wanted to visit the stars ever since we looked up." Max doubted that Rick had understood much of that, so he added. "My ancestors who could not yet make ships and rode horseback wanted to find a way into the stars."

"Query. Clarify horseback."

Max groaned and slid back into the water. His arms were turning to goose flesh in the chilly air anyway. Rather than swimming laps, he did a slow, modified backstroke, enough to keep himself warm. Rick swam next to him, his tentacles graceful in the water. "What about small planets? Shouldn't they be able to reach space easily? They would have light gravity."

"Small planets lack metals of many electrons. They lack..." Rick's explanation devolved into whale song and belches. Whatever small planets lacked, it was more technical than anything Max had taught the computer to translate.

A cramp caught Max under his lowest rib and he rubbed his side as he floated in the water. "So are you saying that all space going species have roughly the same gravity?"

"Limited range, yes. All ships in space have creatures of comparable size and mass. Few outliers at extreme range."

Max thought about the range of alien bodies he'd seen at the space port. He'd seen some that must have topped out at forty or fifty pounds, and others that would probably weigh several hundred if their mass/weight ratios were similar to humans. Now that Max thought about it, that was a limited range. Hell, adult humans had that much variety. The port had lacked any fairy- or dinosaur-sized aliens.

"If everyone evolved on planets with similar gravity, I guess that makes sense. Are there other similarities?"

Several of Rick's tentacles brushed against Max's leg and led certain of Max's parts to pay entirely too much attention. Max made a mental detour into the land of Cornelius Stirk, the psychic cannibal who wanted to eat Batman's heart, and that did the job. The touch of heat in Max's cock vanished, leaving him nothing but gas to worry about. He should get out of the pool before he blew air bubbles of massive proportions and had to explain flatulence.

Rick answered. "All intelligent species have a central point for processing senses—a head. All intelligent life have tentacles."

"Wait a minute." Max flipped back over into a dog paddle. "I'm intelligent, and I don't have tentacles. In fact, a number of tentacle-less aliens were walking around that spaceport."

Rick curled a long tentacle around Max's wrist, lifting it out of the water. "Tentacle," he said.

"Correction. Clarify. Arm," Max responded. Maybe the rest of the universe had tentacles, but red-blooded human beings wouldn't appreciate that particular label.

"Tentacle with interior bone structure."

Max considered that. Rick had a point. Unfortunately. "It resembles a tentacle," Max compromised. He needed to spend some extra time with the translation matrix because if aliens ever bothered visiting the backwoods of Earth, earthlings would get a little cranky over the distinction. At least Americans would. Hell, Max had grown up around people who considered dark skin or sexual orientation tragedies worthy of wailing and a prayer group. Max didn't even want to think how those people would handle tentacles.

Max gasped as another cramp hit.

Rick still had his tentacle curled around Max's wrist, and he pulled their bodies together. "Query. Health?" Even with the translator, Rick's bugling sounded worried. Max's body chose that moment to cramp again, and this time Max let out a giant fart that bubbled up to the surface with a weird smell, like an eraser that had grown hot from too much scrubbing across the paper.

"Human digestive microbes create gas. It sometimes hurts. My health is fine." Max tried to extricate himself from Rick's tentacles. For every one he pulled free, another found a new place to latch onto. Max was not thinking about how the watery wrestling match was causing tentacles to brush over his cock, but he was insanely grateful for cold pool water.

"Query. Assist I in removing gas?"

Max did not even want to think about what Rick might do to get gas out of the intestines. However, whatever plan he came up with, Max preferred to stick with the tried and true method. A little fart party and he'd be fine. "No. It's natural. I appreciate your concern, but I've been dealing with human intestines for a while. Sometimes it's best to let them be gassy."

Rick swam toward the edge of the water, pulling Max with him. "Translation matrix failure."

Max was not getting that message as often as he used to, but it was no less annoying. "I'm healthy. You don't have to worry about me so much. I'm not sure what assumptions you're making about humans, but we're not fragile."

Rick pushed him toward the edge and Max got his feet under him as another bout of gas tried to escape. With Rick guarding the water, Max decided to stage a retreat and find the nearest toilet. As he went for his shirt, Rick followed. "I respect human strength. I would not compensate you for offspring without evidence of human strength. I wish to check health."

Max ignored the request for a checkup. The last thing he needed was a tentacle up his ass. Given the current state of his intestines, that introduced entirely too much opportunity for humiliation. So he changed the subject. "Oh? Are we talking about offspring?" This was the one subject Rick avoided. Most of the time, bringing up the offspring led to Rick's quick retreat, which was evidence of trouble in his domestic life. However, this time Rick hovered near Max, even as Max headed for the door.

"Probability of healthy offspring is high."

"Good. I'm glad to hear it." That was more information than Rick had ever offered on his children up to this point. Max still didn't know how many Rick had, when the ship would pick them up, how old they were, how much care they would require, or even how many eyes they might have. But now he knew they were probably healthy. "When can I see them?"

"Most accepting compensation avoid seeing offspring." Rick had several of his tentacles curled up.

Something was wrong. "That must make it awkward when they're supposed to take care of them."

"Care does not require seeing."

Max narrowed his eyes. If the translation matrix worked well enough for them to have a discussion of the comparative pros and cons of developing a civilization on a large planet, even if it was a rudimentary conversation, they should be able to discuss kids. In fact, Max knew for a fact he had done a whole translation unit on identifying family relationships.

The poor computer had glitched when Max had labeled large numbers of genetic relationships as simply "cousin." He got the feeling that other species liked to have different words to suggest how much genetic material any two individuals shared. Despite once seeing an Internet chart that explained the difference between a third cousin twice removed and a second cousin three times removed, Max couldn't explain any of those more nuanced relationships. So once he got past grandparents, children, siblings and uncles, he pretty much called everything else cousin. Despite all of the time Max had invested in family dynamics, Rick still seemed unable to have a conversation about the children Max was supposed to care for.

"I have a preference for seeing them," Max said slowly. He carefully chose words he knew would be in the translation matrix.

Rick's tentacles curled tighter. "Query. Reason for seeing offspring."

"I don't know. So I know what they look like? I want to look at the children and see if they have your eyes." Max leaned closer.

"They develop their own eyes. They will not require donation of mine."

That had gone right over Rick's head. Max tried again. "I want to see how big the children are. I want to know what they look like. Human offspring have heads and eyes that are larger proportionally. We consider that combination of traits cute."

"Query. Clarify cute."

"Answer. Cute. Causing no harm. Attractive. Inspiring touch." Max had grown strangely good at this game of trying to define things which should not require definition.

A few of Rick's tentacles relaxed a little, but he still looked like a tense little ball of octopus. "All species find offspring of own cute. Humans, no will find my offspring cute."

"Don't bet on it," Max muttered before he organized his words more carefully. "Humans find many offspring cute. We find most offspring cute. Even when offspring are of dangerous predators, humans find them cute."

"Predators are not cute."

"Show me your children."

Rick's tentacles curled up again. The asshole thought Max would hurt them. Max took a step back and tried to rein in his anger. Whatever history Rick's people had with the rest of the aliens, it wasn't good. Hell, Max's alien social worker had hated the idea of Max taking this job. So maybe the babies weren't cute.

Another cramp hit Max's side and he pressed his hand to it and groaned.

Rick darted closer, wrapping his tentacles around Max. "Yes. You see offspring. I check health of offspring and you see."

The pain distracted Max, so Rick was urging him toward the exit before the words filtered down to the important parts of Max's brain. He stopped and nearly pulled Rick off balance. For a second, Rick's considerable weight leaned into Max before he righted himself. "We're going to see the offspring?" Horror swept through Max. "Rick, where are your offspring?"

Rick tilted his head and considered Max out of another grouping of eyes. For a minute, they stared at each other. Then Rick's tentacle slid over Max's wet skin and curled over Max's side. "Offspring here," Rick said.

Fuck. Another cramp struck, and Max gritted his teeth.

"Come. Check health offspring and Max," Rick said, and then he used considerable strength and more speed than Max realized he possessed to hurry Max toward the medical bay. The fucking alien had knocked Max up. Horror washed through him, and his memory provided a montage of chest-bursting aliens. However, Max couldn't imagine Rick allowing his alien kids to kill him. He couldn't. So the horror passed and a healthy dose of anger took its place. As soon as the pain was over, Max definitely would tie one of Rick's tentacles into a knot. He just needed to figure out which tentacle had done the impregnating so he could damage the one that would hurt the most.

Chapter Seven

Max stared at the holographic image of his gut. Or more precisely, he stared at the three blobbish forms that lit up bright white on the scan. Triplets. He was carrying triplets. Fucking aliens. Max had grown to accept many things about aliens. They were illogical. Their ships were claustrophobic. They had a bad habit of putting tentacles where tentacles shouldn't be. But this was the peak of the creepy mountain. He had baby aliens in his gut.

"Offspring difficulty moving." Rick hovered a tentacle near the largest of the three white blobs. The image enlarged, and Max got his first view of the actual alien child. He had his big head pointed up, but only a couple of his short, stubby tentacles pointed down. The rest were shoved in there next to his head, and as Max watched, the offspring wiggled, struggling to get a tentacle free. At the same time, a horrible cramp nearly doubled Max over. He drew his knees up and groaned. "Oh God. Oh God. That does not feel good."

"Offspring turning. Offspring choice for making turn poor."

Max corrected him. "Your offspring is making a poor choice. I agree with that." Max took a deep breath as the pain faded. "He does not have room to be doing yoga." Max wasn't sure he had room to breathe, not that breathing would be a good choice for a creature living in someone's intestines.

As Max watched the screen, the largest tentacles slipped free and eased down into the intestine under the head. Max collapsed back against the bed. "Okay. We need to talk about the word nanny."

"You nanny in return for compensation," Rick said quickly.

Max stared at the boring ceiling. That was much better than watching the alien lifeform on the scanner. He hadn't grown into his tentacles yet, so he was all head and eyes. If the thing were anywhere other than Max's lower intestinal tract, he would call it cute. "This is not nanny. Nanny is protecting offspring after they are born."

Rick was silent for a long time before he said, "Query. Born?"

"Born. Clarification. Outside another's body. Free in the world. Biologically independent." Max was going to spend considerable time in the translation matrix making sure this mistake never, *ever* happened again.

Rick's tentacles drew up. "You nanny for compensation," he repeated.

Max groaned as a smaller cramp rolled through him. Two more small tentacles slipped free of the cramped space up next to the alien head. Now that the largest tentacle was free, apparently the kid would go back to causing normal cramps. Normal. Max needed his head examined if he thought any of this was normal. He probably did need a good examination and a short commitment to a nice place in the country for a "rest."

"Offspring outside is a nanny. Offspring inside is surrogate," Max explained in the simplest terms possible.

"Query. Surrogate?"

"This." Max pointed to his belly and then he pointed to the bright image of the largest of the three children. "This is surrogacy. Your genetic offspring inside my body. Surrogate."

Rick's tentacles quivered and then drew up closer to his body. "Query. Correlation nanny and surrogate?"

"No correlation," Max answered. If anything, he would think that a nanny wouldn't want to be a surrogate because she would want to a connection with her child. But what the hell did Max know? Dark laughter bubbled up when he considered his last Facebook fight with this father. His father was ranting about some new court decision which had made abortion easier, and Max had told him that neither of them got to have an opinion on the matter until they got pregnant. That logic had gone in an unexpected direction now.

Rick's tentacles drew up even farther. The smallest ones were like little balls of tentacle with tiny fingers undulating madly. Max was fairly sure that meant he had an unhappy tentacle monster on his hands. Too fucking bad. If Max was unhappy, he wanted to share his general state of misery, and Rick was the available victim.

He couldn't even go grab a beer and complain with his friends. His friends. That would be a fun conversation. *Hey guys, guess what? I got knocked up by a tentacle monster!* Yeah, that would go over great. Only about half of Max's friends even knew he was gay. Now he was gay and pregnant. Not cool.

Suddenly all of his guilt over turning Rick's medical exam into a sexual encounter vanished. If Rick could run around shoving his offspring into other people, Max could be a pervert who turned a medical exam into a kinky fantasy that made him reconsider his position on tentacles. He was okay with that. He was just not okay with sex leading to pregnancy. That was something straight people had to deal with, not him.

"Query. Surrogate for compensation?" Rick's tentacles were still all little balls of unhappy wiggly fingers.

"Well clearly I am," Max said dryly. This would inspire wild porn if anyone on Earth found out. "I can't say I'm happy. How soon are they going to come out?"

Rick hesitated. "Query. Remove offspring?"

Hope blossomed. "You can remove the offspring?"

Rick stared at him.

With a frustrated sigh, Max rephrased his question. "Query. Can you remove offspring?"

"Yes."

That was rather literal. Max felt like he was having a conversation with his ninth grade English teacher who refused to let anyone use the bathroom unless they said, *may I* instead of *can I*.

"Query. Will you remove offspring?"

For several minutes, Rick did not answer. That was Max's first indication that something was wrong. Usually, Rick enjoyed conversations, even when he did not understand what Max was saying. He was a laid-back guy that way. Max frowned. Wait. Rick wasn't laid-back. He was overprotective. The fucker had been keeping track of Max because Max was pregnant with his children. Max had a moment where his brain reassembled itself, and when it was done, he liked Rick a little bit less.

"Answer. I can," Rick finally said.

He could, but he wasn't offering to. Max was not a stupid man, and he had made a few connections.

He sat up. "Query. Can offspring come out?"

Rick turned to the hatch that Max associated with medical equipment. "Answer. Yes. No damage to Max." Rick had retreated to a formality and simplicity in language that the translator could handle. No temporary failures and whale song or belches. Just simple, cold fact.

"Query. Damage to children?" Max asked.

Rick turned and he held a silver and blue tennis racket looking thing with one tentacle. Rick walked over to the active scanner image and used a tentacle to poke right in the middle of the figure of the tiny gymnast octopus currently trying to do somersaults in Max's gut.

"Likely to survive. Might not." That included a number of whistle sounds the translator missed.

"Query. Will the other two survive?" Max had a horrible feeling in his gut.

"Clarification. Smaller two offspring..." The translator failed again, but Max was a bright guy. He got what Rick was trying to say.

Max hated the way he felt, and he didn't want aliens in his gut, but he didn't want those lives gone because a fucking computer had mistranslated nanny and Rick hadn't kept his tentacles to himself. Max gripped the edge of the med bay bed so hard that his forearms trembled. He assumed Rick felt equally bad because most of his tentacles were still drawn up tight. The whole of his walking tentacle was visible in its pale fleshy color. A hint of the orange-red showed on one side. Max looked at that rather than at the silver instrument.

After a painfully long silence, Rick asked, "Query. Remove all I offspring now?"

Max opened his mouth, but words didn't come out. He wanted to say he'd never been pregnant. He didn't want to be the cause of Rick's triplets dying. But he wanted them alive somewhere else, which was impossible, because they were in him.

Max's brain started spinning in a circle. His brain and Rick's oldest child were equally fond of spinning and turning in spaces that were far too small for that. Rick inched closer with that silver instrument, and Max scooted backwards without making a conscious choice.

"I can't do this," Max said softly.

"Understood. Removal of children is optimal." Despite his words, Rick's tentacles were still balled up and his finger tentacles waved like leaves in a high wind. Correction, in a hurricane.

When Rick reached out a tentacle, Max slid off the far side of the table. "No. I mean I can't do this now. I can't make this decision now." Max couldn't explain what was going on in his head. Hell, even if he'd had another English speaker around, he still wouldn't have the words. It would take a team of psychiatrists to drag anything coherent out of his brain. So instead, Max turned and fled from the room. His last view of the medical scanner was of the largest offspring, slipping two more tentacles free.

Instead of going back to his quarters, Max headed for a hatch that led into a network of crawl spaces that crisscrossed the spaces between decks. He had found it early in his explorations, and he liked the privacy. Rick was large, and Max hoped he couldn't fit into the narrow passage. As an octopusish alien, he could probably squeeze himself into impossible shapes, but right now Max wanted the illusion that he could escape.

He climbed the peg ladder into the shaft and ignored the possibility that Rick could reach him or use the ship scanners to find him. The military was far too frugal to install internal sensors with the ability to track individuals, and Max hoped aliens had the same streak of cheap.

When he reached the first junction, he scooted around and let his legs dangle over the edge. The other possibility was that this was some sort of venting system and Max was exposing himself to alien radiation, but he didn't worry about that too much now. If this were dangerous, Rick would have stopped him.

Fuck.

Max had started to think of Rick as a friend, a lonely alien bachelor whose mate had taken off with the kids. He had liked Rick. Really liked him. Max was an idiot. Officially.

He leaned against the side of the shaft and rested his hand over the area where he kept getting cramps. "It was you the whole time. You think you're Kohei Uchimura in there, don't you?" Max asked. "Well he had an Olympic mat for his routine. You need to stop your tumbling practice in my gut, you little monster," Max said as he rubbed his side. "Your dad is going to have his tentacles full with you."

Max frowned. If Rick was the dad, where was the mom? Maybe he was being too Earth-centric in his thinking, but he assumed complex creatures needed sexual reproduction. Asexual reproduction was nature's form of cloning which would not allow adaptation. At least that's what Max had learned in his biology courses in school, not that his biology teachers had a whole lot of experience with tentacle monsters. So maybe he should stop assuming he understood anything. Clearly he didn't understand the word nanny.

Another cramp hit, but it was a small one that Max would have dismissed as gas a few hours ago. Hell, he had been dismissing the random pains as gas. "Will your siblings get this active or are you the pushy one?" Max's mother always talked about how much easier her second pregnancy had been because Max had turned and stretched and rammed his head into her cervix and given her false labor pains and generally made her life a living nightmare.

Max didn't think he should pay for anything he had done pre-birth, but she still sometimes brought it up when she was annoyed with him. "Don't you even start," she'd say. "You've been giving me grief since you were six months in the womb and you started head-butting my cervix."

Max wondered if he would see her again. As a realist, he knew that four years was a long time. And now that Max knew Rick wanted him as a surrogate, it wasn't likely this job would last that long. So his dream of getting a ticket home was just that... a dream. He would provide Rick with three offspring and then Rick would drop him off on the next planet.

He wondered if he would rate a social worker the second time around. Honestly, he needed the help because he got himself in trouble when left on his own.

"I don't blame you for this," he told all three offspring as he rubbed his stomach, "but this situation sucks. And I can't blame your father. He's a pretty decent guy, and he loves the hell out of you three. He hangs over me like an umbrella every time I do anything physical." Weirdly, a jab of jealousy stabbed him.

"I should be the adult and go talk to him." Instead Max sat in the shaft and stared at nothing. He couldn't gather the energy for anything else.

Chapter Eight

After an hour of staring at a computer that kept screeching for attention when Max didn't answer translation questions, Max gave up and headed for the swimming room. Rick had been so insistent that swimming was healthy. That should have been some sort of sign, but no. Max had assumed that Rick wanted to be helpful.

Helpful like shoving his baby-making tentacle up Max's ass. Max wasn't particularly body-conscious, but as he stripped out of his clothes, he ran a hand over his stomach. He felt the slight bulge where Kohei was hiding. "If you hadn't tried to do somersaults, who knows how long it would have taken me to figure this out." Too damn long.

Max slipped into the water, shivering at the cold before swimming toward the tiny water circulation islands where the water was warmer. Max was still swimming an hour or so later when Rick slipped into the room and hovered near the door. If Max had been mature, he would've swam over and had an adult conversation with the tentacle monster who had knocked him up. He would. However, he felt like sulking.

Rick slid forward, strangely graceful on his single central leg. At the edge of the pool, he stopped, and one tentacle spasmed. "Query," Rick said, and then the translator failed, emitting a series of whale songs and whistles that Max would not have even recognized as a language before leaving Earth.

They needed to have this conversation, whether Max wanted it or not. At least Rick was polite enough to keep a distance. Max caught the edge of one of the islands and propped his elbows on it so he could watch Rick. "Translation matrix fail."

"Query...." For a second time the translator failed.

Max had to take control of the conversation or Rick might break his translator with all the untranslatable phrases. Max assumed the big dork was trying to talk about feelings. And normally Max was in favor of that. He avoided embracing the stereotype of repressed military man who killed himself by drinking his emotions. He'd seen friends do that after leaving combat.

But right now Max couldn't handle getting in touch with his emotions, in part because he didn't know what he was feeling. Maybe women imagined themselves pregnant—he'd never asked. But he hadn't. He'd had fantasies about winning the lottery, and nightmares about getting shot down behind enemy lines and surviving long enough to get captured. He'd mentally rehearsed pickup lines and wondered what it would feel like if his little brother died. That last one was sort of shitty, but in his defense, Pete was a pain in his ass. Generally, these sorts of morbid thoughts led to some intense discomfort, followed by immense gratitude that he didn't have to deal with them.

He'd even developed elaborate murder plots for his ex-boyfriend—he-who-shall-not-be-named. The little troll deserved a good killing, but Max valued his freedom too much, and maybe there was a little nagging thought of the immorality of murder holding him back as well. Just a little one.

However, he had never indulged in a pregnancy fantasy—not in a dream or a nightmare. Not unless he counted the nightmares after watching *Alien* for the first time, but Max hoped that didn't count. Rick seemed confident that being a surrogate wouldn't harm Max, and the social worker would have stopped him from signing up for a suicide job. Hopefully. Shit. Now Max's imagination was circling an unhappy place.

"Query. Will being the surrogate harm my health?" Max asked.

Rick's tentacles quivered and then drew up. "Provide discomfort.... Stretching of skin... and muscles. Well within tolerances." A few descriptions in the middle failed to make it through the translator, but Max got the general idea. Being pregnant wouldn't kill him. Max was surprised the kids were able to survive because intestines seemed like an inhospitable place to grow. Rick slid forward and gave another long string of untranslatable words; the translator caught "offspring" and "remove."

If Max's kids were in some woman who was considering abortion, he would feel something, too. Of course he would avoid getting someone pregnant if he didn't speak the same language, and being gay, that was a bit of a moot point. Gay couples had to jump through more hoops to get kids. Only hets produced sentient life by accident.

"I will be surrogate in return for compensation," Max said. Rick's tentacles uncurled and two waved. He had one hell of a bad poker face. Or poker extremities, anyway.

"Query. Time given for surrogate in return for compensation?"

Oh Lord. Here they went again with time. Max had no idea how Heetayu's computer could translate years and Rick's couldn't. Hell, when he did an audio search for "seconds," he got television broadcasts where people said, "Wait a second" or "Do you want seconds?" Minutes and hours had been equally unhelpful. He frowned. Wait. The ground had been counting down to a Patriot missile launch. The mission had been to keep the ships away from the populated areas until the SAM system was in place.

Max did a fast breaststroke toward the edge of the pool, and Rick retreated damn fast for an octopus with one leg. He even got a couple of his longer tentacles involved, but Max ignored him. He grabbed clothes on the way past, and dried himself with them as he ran bare assed naked toward the translation room.

Rick probably had another name for the computer cubby, but Max had taken the space over for his translation work, and Rick hadn't cared.

"Computer," Max said as he slapped his wet hand down on the identification screen. "Search Earth broadcasts for phrase 'T-minus.'" Max struggled into his pants. The fabric clung to his wet skin, and Max shook his leg to get it to slide into the pants. He then had to hop as he switched feet.

The computer speaker immediately broadcast the audio Max remembered. He'd been in his jet, focused on the ship in front of him. If the Patriot missile had taken him down, he wouldn't have cared as long as it had destroyed the aliens. The memory of that helpless rage swelled up as he listened to the recording of the controller's voice. "T-minus forty-five... forty-four... forty-three... forty-two..." The voice got to twenty-three before Max said, "Stop!" The countdown had been somewhere around eight or ten when Max had lost consciousness.

And the whole damn alien invasion had been nothing more than a police chase. How many people had died from battle debris falling to the ground? Max wondered whether his own plane or that Patriot missile had fallen to Earth and killed even more. Max's stomach cramped as Kohei did something unfortunately athletic.

"Right, right. No upsetting the babies." Max rubbed his side and sat on the stool. Maybe Kohei had the ability to sense emotion through some chemical in Max's body. It would help if he understood alien biology, but at this point, Max would settle for sorting out the time issue. The dock computer system and Rick's computers were not great at sharing information. Yet the raw transmissions from the government's fly-by of Earth were all available. Politics must be involved. But he couldn't worry about that right now.

A squelch announced Rick's arrival. Any time he got his walking tentacle wet, it made unfortunate noises on the padded floor. Max ignored it because the one question they each wanted answered required the computer to sort out time markers.

"Computer, mark the sequence of numbers."

"Marked."

"The speaker is counting down seconds. Use the time intervals between T-minus forty-five and T-minus fifteen to define thirty seconds." Max pulled the damn shirt over his head.

Maybe it was Max's imagination, but the computer took more time than appropriate, as if it was frustrated with Max's questionable translation skills. "Thirty seconds, confirm. Require secondary confirmation."

"Use the length of time between T-minus forty and T-minus ten."

Again, the computer paused. Whenever they had attempted to define time, this was where the computer called him an idiot because his first time interval didn't match his second. This time the computer said, "Deviation within acceptable boundaries. External source required for confirmation."

Fuck. If Max tried to do the one-Mississippi, two-Mississippi thing again, he would screw it up and they'd be back at square zero. He rubbed his stomach. Thirty seconds. He needed something that would correlate to thirty seconds. He smiled. "Check the entertainment broadcasts. They are interrupted by persuasive and informational transmissions. Traditionally, those interrupting transmissions are either thirty or sixty seconds."

"Confirm correlation between persuasive and informational transmissions and commercials," the computer asked.

"High correlation," Max said. The computer began running through commercials so quickly that Max could barely recognize a few famous jingles played at supersonic speeds. Then the computer went silent. "Unit one second confirmed," the computer said. Max almost wept with joy. He pushed the emotions aside and focused on using that one unit to explain time units in English. Sixty seconds in a minute.

Sixty minutes in an hour. Twenty-four hours in a day. Three hundred and sixty five and a quarter days in a year. One-twelfth of a year in a month. Max stopped there. If he needed to count time in decades, he was throwing himself out an airlock. Just as soon as he found one.

The computer tried to restart a number of time-related questions regarding human lifespan and development, but Max slapped his hand on the master control to shut it down in the middle of a word. Then he turned around to face Rick.

"Query. Remaining time for surrogacy of offspring."

Rick inched closer. "Clarify. Minimum time of survival, optimal time of survival, required time for compensation or average time based on biological precedent?"

That was an excellent question. Well Max had never done a job half-assed in his life, at least not after that one summer when he'd been stupid enough to think that a lawn-mowing job in the heat was a good idea. "Optimal time of survival," Max said.

Rick relaxed so much that he shrank a couple of inches as his central tentacle sagged. This time when Rick gave his whale song, the translator offered, "Six and three quarter months."

Max rubbed his stomach. "Query. Will all offspring come out at once?" It sure seemed like Kohei was more developed than his siblings.

Rick rotated clockwise a half turn. "If large offspring must pass smaller offspring, then smaller offspring are pushed out."

That meant that they might appear at different times. Max was still a little worried about what happened when the offspring were large enough to create a blockage, but for now, he would assume that if Rick's species went around shoving eggs up other creature's asses they knew how to do it without causing harm.

"Query." Rick said slowly. The translator might use a constant speed, but the belch Rick used for that word was cartoonish in length. "Surrogate for compensation?"

"Yes," Max said. "Surrogate for compensation. I should make you drive me home afterward."

"Clarify. Home."

Max almost cried. Some sadistic part of him wanted to confuse Rick by defining it as the place Max would never see again. It would be like the liar's paradox during a *Star Trek* episode. One of the crew, either Spock or Kirk, had told an android that Mudd could only tell lies. Mudd then announced, "I am lying." Max wondered if it would send Rick into the same sort of tailspin if Max told him to take Max home and then defined home as a place he would never see. However, the more logical part of him knew that Rick had never meant to lie to Max or even confuse him. In his alien, octopussy way, he'd been as honest as he could.

"It's a place where a person belongs," Max said. He didn't know if that would translate, but clearly Rick had understood some part of it.

Rick rushed to say, "Agreed. I will return you to Central Trading City Nineteen-Sector Twelve."

Max blinked. Rick's offer was perverse. Well-intentioned, but no less painful for all his altruism. At least Max knew there would be computers he could use and a central government organized enough to send out social workers for randomly kidnapped members of pre-space flight civilizations. "Okay." Max stared at Rick, not sure what to say after that. For the first time since he came on the ship, he felt like an employee or maybe a junior officer trapped in a room with a general.

Rick did another quarter turn. "Query. Correlation humans and willingness to surrogate for compensation."

Max leaned against the computer. The sloping chairs weren't comfortable, but he didn't want to stand as if Rick were a superior officer. Nope. He wasn't. He was Max's boss... and the father of the children Max was carrying. Max was *so* going to need boatloads of therapy. Big old super freighters full of the stuff. And booze. Lots of booze. "It's not common, but some human females cannot carry their own young, so others will carry the child for them."

"Query. Surrogate for compensation?"

"Some of them, yes."

"Query. Correlate surrogate and female?"

Max almost laughed. Until two hours ago, he would have said there was a one hundred percent correlation, but apparently not. "Human females carry offspring. Human males do not."

"Query. Max male or female?"

Max sighed. "Don't emasculate me anymore than you already have. I'm a male." Max figured the translator would miss most of that, and he didn't want the translator to serve up all of Max's feelings on a silver platter. Sometimes Max needed to complain out loud without running the risk of pissing off his boss. On the good side, he couldn't exactly get fired.

"Query," Max asked. "Do all offspring of your species grow in animals of other species?"

"Yes. Carrying offspring is biologically wearying."

That was a properly logical answer. Max was surprised Vulcans hadn't come up with the solution, although that would have made the *Star Trek* universe weirdly kinky. Max wasn't sure the 1960s had been ready for that. And if Rick's two younger kids took after their big brother in the athletics department, wearying would be a bit of an understatement.

"Clarify. Regret translation matrix failure," Rick said.

Regret. That was the one emotion Max had managed to get the translation computer to understand. When something broke, the response was regret. If something tasted bad, it created regret. If an alien accidentally knocked up a male of another species without warning, apparently that was regret as well.

"It's fine," Max said, even though it wasn't.

Rick inched closer, and a tentacle brushed against Max's arm. "Regret causing of distress. Max is pleasant and interesting male individual."

It was still the nicest apology Max had gotten in a while.

Chapter Nine

Max floated in the pool. Since he had convinced Rick to raise the temperature a few degrees, it was much more comfortable. And as a bonus, certain body parts no longer had to suffer embarrassing shrinkage.

The door opened, and Max tilted his head to watch Rick slide into the room. A cramp struck, and Max rubbed the huge lump above his hip bone. Kohei had grown a lot in the last five months, and now his brother was large enough to create a second lump. Weirdly, Max looked sorta pregnant. He also looked a little like a cartoon snake that had swallowed a bird and the shape of the bird was still visible through his stomach. Sometimes the Kohei lump even moved. And pain had become a constant companion.

Considering that these two had already caused more discomfort than basic training, Max was surprised by how much he worried about them. Even Rick admitted that they were growing faster than anticipated and they would likely come out early. Rick slid his hat off and set it aside. One good splash fight and Rick had decided to avoid exposing his tools to that sort of soaking.

Rick swam closer. He was so graceful in the water with his undulating tentacles, and Max was even getting used to the weird and random eye placement. "Query. How is your health?"

"It kind of sucks." Max rubbed his protruding Kohei bulge. The cramps had passed too-much-bad-Mexican-food and entered into holy-crap-I think-I-might-need-to-visit-the-hospital territory. At this point, Max had some unpleasant thoughts about those chest bursting aliens that showed up in so many science fiction B-movies he had watched as a kid. The 80s had been obsessed with things bursting out of bodies. A whole generation of children had been traumatized by fake blood and cheesy aliens.

"Offspring arrive soon." Rick started swimming around Max in lazy circles. Max closed his eyes and floated. Rick had started this weird ritual about a month ago, and it reminded him a little of those videos where fish swam around and around to disturb the sand into fancy patterns to attract a mate. Considering Rick's species had used non-sentient species to carry their young in the past, it was probably some sort of instinct to make sure the host surrogate didn't eat the children.

Host surrogate. Max still had trouble wrapping his head around the idea. It would be like his mother deciding that carrying children was too much hassle and having the family dog do it for her. Max might not tell Rick, but he understood why other aliens had a problem with Rick's species and their weird reproductive habits. That division between Rick's people and others had to be pretty deep too. When Max had tried to get the name of Rick's species, he had only been able to call his own people, "People." But when Max had asked what others called them, all the tentacles had curled up like an octopus on a hot griddle.

"I'm concerned about how the offspring plan on arriving," Max said. He'd been avoiding that question ever since Rick made the big announcement, but Max needed to put on his big boy pants and face the truth.

"Translation matrix failure. Query. Clarify."

The translator was so much better after months of work, but they would still run into trouble in the weirdest spots. "Query," Max said. "Will offspring damage me?" Rick had reassured him a number of times, but considering how large the children lumps were getting, Max needed to hear it again.

"No damage. Discomfort. Max good, safe, male surrogate." Rick was cute in his attempt to say the right words, even when he didn't understand them. However, Max's complaints about his masculinity inspired Rick to reaffirm Max's gender on a semi-regular basis.

Max rubbed his stomach. If this was discomfort, Max did not want to see what Rick would define as pain. If he ever got home to earth, he needed to buy his mother the biggest box of chocolates he could find. Having a living, squirming being inside his guts was not a comfortable feeling. And right now Max felt guilty about every time he'd kicked her bladder.

"Query. Does Max feel damaged?" Tentacles brushed across Max's stomach.

Max twisted and flailed in the water, and that woke Kohei, who immediately started writing in his guts. For a half second, Max thought he would go under the water, but then tentacles curled around him, pulling him tight up against Rick's body. Surprise made Max gasp. Rick was warm, far warmer than Max had expected, given that his tentacles ran on the cool side. "Query. I remove you from the water?"

"No. I'm fine. You startled me." Max tried to pull away, but Rick held on. Max had an ex-boyfriend or two who had gotten pretty handsy, but nothing prepared him to deal with dozens of tentacles all wrapping around him at once.

"Query. Clarify startled."

"You moved too quickly or touched me unexpectedly, and my muscles reacted before I made a decision to react."

"Query. Correlation startle with fight. Correlation startle with flee."

Max snorted. Of course that's where Rick's big brain went first. He was all worried that Max's instincts would make him hide when the pain of childbirth kicked in. Max had survived a basic training accident where his main parachute hadn't fully deployed. The backup had worked as designed, but the extra time in freefall and an unanticipated wind had blown him into a wooded area where he'd impaled his leg on a broken tree limb. If he had survived that, he wouldn't get illogical about a baby octopus crawling out his ass.

"I won't flee. 'Startle' doesn't correlate with either. And if I were going to run when I hurt, I would already be racing out of the room. I feel like someone has taken a large rock and hit me in the stomach several times."

Several of Rick's tentacles shriveled up into unhappy little balls. "The water is nutrient rich. I have overfed offspring."

Max peeled the remaining few tentacles from his arms and pushed away. Part of him didn't want to because Rick was deliciously warm and squishy. He was like a big bean bag, a hot water bottle, and a body pillow had a kinky threesome. The fact that Max enjoyed his comfort was the biggest reason to avoid it. He couldn't afford to rely emotionally on Rick. "So that's why you always encouraged me to go swimming. These nutrients aren't anything gross, are they?" Max hoped he wasn't swimming in the alien version of mother's milk.

"Query. Clarify gross." Rick withdrew his tentacles and allowed Max to swim free, but he kept pace with him and swam close enough to be within tentacle reach.

There were so many ways that Max could've answered. However, he chose to go with the definition that concerned him the most. "Clarification. Gross: relating to the bodily fluids of another. Occasionally, relating to one's own bodily fluids if they are fluids that one would rather have on the inside of one's body."

Max could remember once or twice when he had been particularly gross. As a young man, most of those cases involved alcohol not alien impregnation. Of course the leg impaling incident had also been a little gross. Both blood and urine had been involved, and the medic's attempt to reassure him by explaining how peeing was natural had traumatized him more. Having someone compare him to a gazelle that peed itself when getting chased by a lion had not restored his dignity.

Rick's tentacles slowly uncurled. "Water is not gross."

"Well that's good. So now I just have to worry that your child appears to be trying to crawl out of my bellybutton."

"Clarify bellybutton."

Max touched his own stomach where his outie bellybutton was on display, since he had so far failed to explain bathing suit in adequate terms. It was also possible that Rick understood what a bathing suit was, but simply thought it was stupid. Either way, Max had grown used to skinny-dipping. "This is a bellybutton."

Rick brushed a tentacle across Max's stomach. "Bellybutton lacks internal channel to intestinal tract."

"I know."

"Query. Offspring cannot appear through bellybutton."

Max sighed. "Answer. Exaggeration in order to emphasize an argument." Max was getting frighteningly good at these verbal games. He felt like he should earn a merit badge in annoying alien linguistics.

"Query. What argument are you making?"

"Answer. Offspring cause pain."

A flurry of air bubbles came out from under Rick's mantle of tentacles. Either that was an alien sigh, or farting was how Rick expressed frustration. Who knew? After the bubbles stopped, Rick said, "I regret offspring cause pain."

"Thank you, and I accept your apology, but I still hurt."

Rick used his largest tentacle to stroke the Kohei bump. "Offspring arrive soon."

Max frowned. Rick didn't make mistakes conjugating his verbs anymore, not unless he was trying to talk about things that might have been but weren't. Rick and his computer both sucked at translating *might haves*. No doubt a linguist could've drawn some deep, meaningful conclusions from that. However, Rick's verb implied that more than one kid might come out. Kohei was ready. Given the way Max's stomach had formed unnatural bulges, the second child might be ready even if he was smaller, but Max had yet to see anything from the third child. Thing One and Thing Two made visible bumps that caused localized cramping, but Thing Three was still too small to do either. "Query. Number of offspring that will arrive soon."

"Query. Clarify soon." Maybe Max was imagining it, but that seemed like an evasive answer. Max groaned as another cramp hit him. If *soon* wasn't within the next few hours, or at the very least the next few days, Max might give himself a cesarean.

"Query. When will first offspring arrive?" Max asked.

"Zero to six hours."

Relief slapped Max right across the pregnant stomach. "Oh thank God. Query. Will other offspring appear within zero to six hours?"

"Unknown." Strangely, Rick's tentacles now drew up tightly.

Max frowned. "Query. Should other offspring appear?"

Rick swam backward, taking him farther away from Max. "I dislike ambiguity of the term 'should.'"

"Okay, now you're playing word games with me. So why don't you ignore your personal feelings about the English language and tell me what will happen if other offspring appear soon."

Rick took up his circling sentry duty again. "I am unable to predict future."

"Define probabilities," Max challenged him.

"Probability." After saying that word, Rick fell silent. No way had the computer mistranslated it. The damn thing adored using that word to test Max's understanding of technology. It would show him a picture of a ship approaching a space station or an asteroid or a planet and then ask for probable outcomes. Max had learned that the computer had a diverse and disturbingly creative algorithms for ways a pilot could crash his ship. After a time, Rick answered. "Second offspring will appear soon after first. Development has been more rapid than anticipated."

The tension in his tentacles suggested that Rick didn't like the answer. "Query. Do offspring usually appear one at a time?"

"Yes."

Max waited. Rick was uncomfortable talking about reproduction, and Max had learned that patience worked better than verbal sparring. Rick might play dumb, but he knew how to misinterpret questions and get the conversation off track. He was a master at it. After another long pause, Rick continued. "First offspring appears days or weeks first. It helps to care for other offspring, or in the case of nutrient shortage, cannibalizes other offspring."

Max stopped swimming. Immediately Rick was there at his side, tentacles reaching out, but Max swam backward. "You had better tell me that there are a lot of nutrients on this ship, because if these children eat each other, I will not be happy." Max's stomach rolled at the idea. At least now Max knew why the computer had included cannibalism in a lesson that had defined herbivore, carnivore, and rock-eating. At the time, Max had suspected that some bored linguist had been fucking with newcomers. Apparently not.

"Offspring being cannibalized is not optimal."

"If you had any other opinion on the issue, I would take two of your tentacles and tie them in a knot," Max said. Then he pointed at Rick. "And I would pick important tentacles."

Splashing, Rick made a comical production out of shifting his tentacles to a more protected position on the other side of his big bulbous head. However, he couldn't feel too threatened because he continued to float right next to Max. "Pool has excess of nutrients. Arrival of two offspring will not result in lack of nourishment."

Max frowned. "Query. Is there enough nutrition for three offspring?"

"Nutrients in sufficient quantity for three offspring."

Max didn't need a secret decoder ring to figure out what Rick wasn't saying. The two bulges in his stomach were enough to suggest there was a problem. Max lacked subtlety so he came right out and asked, "Query. Is third offspring large enough to survive?"

"Unknown." The computer's translated voice sounded so unemotional and factual, but Rick's tentacles drew up into spiral curly fries of unhappiness. Max had never planned to have children, and if he had, adoption would have been choice number one, with surrogacy and fostering two and three on the list. Alien impregnation was not something he had ever contemplated. But now that he was pregnant, he was surprisingly upset at the idea that one offspring was too small. "Query. Will small offspring remain inside?"

"When two offspring arrive, digestive tract is wide and flooded with hormone signal to arrive arrive arrive," Rick said. His words grew faster. "Third offspring may arrive early."

Max caught the edge of a filter island and pulled himself upright. "Do you have medical equipment for a premature birth?"

"Translation matrix failure. Clarify."

"Birth. Clarify. The arrival of offspring. The pain involved in arrival of offspring."

"Query. Why would human females continue to carry offspring if to carry offspring is to suffer pain?" Rick asked. It was a classic change of topic, but Rick's refusal to answer told Max what he needed to know. His guts ached. He didn't want any of the children to die, but if Rick didn't know how to help, there wasn't much Max could do. But upsetting Rick even more didn't seem kind, not when his tentacles were all kinked and curled.

"Humans like sex," Max said. He immediately corrected himself. "Almost all of us like sex. It's fun."

Rick stopped circling and started his undulating version of a dog paddle. "The creation of offspring is entertaining?"

"Very. And women like to be entertained just as much as men."

"The value of entertainment is greater than the distress of pain. Interesting."

"And untrue," Max said. "The pain is greater than the entertainment." Max wasn't sure if that was true for women, but he found that his one blissful and erotic encounter with Rick's eggy tentacle didn't make up for months of gas, stomach pain, vomiting, cramping, and general misery.

"Carrying offspring is illogical."

"But people like offspring. They want offspring. If the only way for you to have offspring was for you to carry it yourself, wouldn't you?" Max asked. Rick didn't answer, and it occurred to Max that Rick might not have the right equipment. If Max ignored Rick's many tentacles, the trunk of his body was significantly smaller than a human's. His walking tentacle was so long that Rick appeared to be larger, but his body was small. He might not have a digestive tract long enough to give the children space to grow.

"I am unsure," Rick said. "Offspring cause pain. I would rather compensate another."

Max rubbed his largest bulge. "I can see why. Your children are large."

"Yes. The size of offspring and manner of incubation is gross and distasteful to other species."

Considering that Max had defined gross as involving bodily fluids, Max chose to ignore that part of the statement. No doubt Max's body contained all sorts of alien fluids, but denial was his happy place right now. "Do other species bear their own offspring?"

"Many prefer external fertilization and growth within protective barriers."

"Eggs," Max translated. "They lay eggs. Right now, I'm thinking that might be a biologically smart move." A stronger cramp rippled through his gut, and Max clung to the water circulation island.

"Offspring come," Rick said. Tentacles wrapped around Max's limbs. Max might have complained, but the strongest cramp yet hit him. Max cried out and curled his legs up as white-hot pain seared his nerves.

Chapter Ten

Max groaned as Rick helped him onto the table. "On your stomach will make exit easier for offspring to exit."

"I don't think I should lie on my stomach," Max said, but he didn't make any other protest as Rick encouraged him to roll over. Much to his surprise, the cramps didn't get worse as he settled on his stomach. "Query. Is it supposed to hurt this much?"

"No." Rick hurried to the nook and pulled out several instruments. They were quickly leaving the land of kinky porn and approaching horror flicks. "Offspring may be struggling to get free. Human intestines are anomalously circuitous," Rick explained.

Circuitous. That was not a term Max would've ever chosen, but it communicated a clear and terrifying reality. "Clarify. By struggling, are you suggesting that your offspring is about to rip my intestine?" Max held his breath.

"Negative. Offspring do not damage the carrier," Rick said immediately. Maybe Max was imagining it, but he almost sounded offended. "They may sometimes hurt the carrier," Rick then admitted. "I can ease the way for the offspring to minimize pain."

Max pressed his forehead to the table and clutched the edge as pain rolled through him. "Minimize pain. That would be awesome. Do that."

Tentacles pulled Max's legs apart, but he didn't care. Shame and titillation both vanished under the need to focus through the pain.

Max panted as the tentacle slid inside. "I shall attempt to avoid activating reproductive system," Rick said.

Max gave a rough bark of laughter. "Oh trust me, there is zero chance of my reproductive system getting activated."

Rick paused, and Max arched his back as Kohei made his presence known again. If he kept this up, Max was taking the snot-nosed bastard off the Christmas card list. Rick's tentacle slid inside again, stretching Max's hole. This time the uncomfortable feeling was nothing more than a welcome distraction. Rick said, "Clarify. I believed I had triggered reproduction when I implanted offspring."

"You did, but touch alone does not activate the reproductive system," Max said through clenched teeth. Part of him wanted to tell Rick to shut the fuck up, but another part wanted some distraction from the pain in his body, and awkward conversation qualified as something. "When I'm in this much pain, I have no interest in any sort of reproductive entertainment."

"Human biology is confusing."

"You are the species that puts offspring in other species, so I don't think you get to call me strange."

"Species of mine is strange as well." Rick made an odd huffing noise. "We do not gain approval from others."

Max was proud of himself for not pointing out that a certain subset of humanity would approve of Rick's whole reproductive scheme. They bought tentacle sex toys like the one that had sent Max running the opposite direction. He'd gotten into a fight with his ex about that damn toy, and now Max had dirty little fantasies about what Rick could do if there weren't children up there. Maybe Max would have been more adventurous if his other partners had shown half of Rick's patience.

"Get in there and help the offspring out," Max said.

"I shall." Rick had a strangely formal cadence to his voice, even in his weird belchy voice. "Try and relax." Rick devoted a couple of tentacles to rubbing Max's lower back.

"That's *try to relax*, and that's not easy when baby octopuses are doing gymnastics routines in my large intestine."

Rick continued the tentacle massage. "The computer suggests that you use the additive conjunction *and* more often than the directional preposition *to* after the word *try*."

Max narrowed his eyes. "Are you giving me shit about my English? Seriously?"

"I am most often serious."

Laughter burst out so unexpectedly that Max snorted. He hadn't pulled that sort of dork move since middle school, but luckily aliens didn't recognize goofy laughter. The largest cramp yet hit, and Max arched his back and bit back a scream as the skin over his side rippled. Someone's tentacle had hit a sensitive spot. "Oh God. Oh God. I think I'm about to have an accident on the floor."

Rick's tentacles tightened around his waist. "I shall not allow you to fall." It took Max several seconds to realize that Rick had misunderstood.

"Clarify. In this context, accident means something gross." Max was grateful he had already defined that word.

"If bodily fluids appear, it is an involuntary reaction and not an accident as you have defined it, unless humans have more control over bodily fluids than other species."

"Clearly not because I'm about to poop on you."

Rick's calm, "That is highly unlikely," was oddly comforting. However, Max had suffered some pretty gnarly diarrhea lately.

A cramp rippled through his stomach and he cried out as something wet flowed down the back of his legs. "Oh, shit."

"It is not shit. It is nutrient fluid absorbed from the swimming."

Max struggled to look over his shoulder. "I absorbed the pool water?" Rick had a tentacle all the way up Max's ass, and if it weren't for the horrific pain, Max would have considered the image some nice wank material, right up there with Sherlock and John getting themselves handcuffed together before going on the run from the law.

"Clarification. The offspring absorbed fluid and created a nutrient pouch. But the membrane has ruptured and the offspring must come out."

Max mentally translated that to *his water had broken*. Then he arched his back as another series of cramps seized his body so he couldn't speak. One of Rick's tentacles slid across his face, cooling him.

"They better come out soon."

"They will can. I regret the pain my offspring cause." Rick hesitated. "I regret the pain I caused in overfeeding my offspring."

"As long as everyone separates without anyone being torn in half, we can call it good. Now please help them out."

Rick went to the wall, his tentacle slipping almost all the way out of Max's body. Despite Max's earlier comment, his cock did notice that. Luckily another cramp hit before the moronic organ could do something that would humiliate him. The air over Max shimmered before displaying alien text that floated in space.

Rick returned, and Max gasped as the tentacle pushed back inside. "The largest offspring is nearly out now."

"Oh shit." The pressure against Max's asshole was like nothing he'd ever felt before. Skin stretched and stung and muscles strained until every instinct Max possessed told him to push. But his butt was not a vagina. Max suspected that pushing would do serious damage, so he fought the urge and forced his legs to relax. "Hurry up."

"The first offspring is bulky."

"I do realize that." Max's voice first rose to an unmanly squeak and then broke. He had to take a deep breath before continuing. "However, I can't control my muscles forever."

"Query. Clarify control muscles."

Max's ass burned like the first time he'd experimented with a butt plug and hadn't known that if a young idiot left it in and allowed the lube to get absorbed, pulling it back out would become an exercise in masochism. "Clarification. I want to bear down and tighten all the muscles around the obstruction. I'm thinking that's a human reaction to having something too large pass through. Just clench the muscles and it all gets compacted tighter." Max had no idea if that was true or not, but it seemed plausible because his body was screaming at him to clench hard.

"I shall endeavor to expedite the offspring," Rick said. He pushed his tentacle in, and Max squealed. "Observe. Offspring is nearly past the last bend." Rick changed the holographic image above Max. It now showed a grayscale close up of his intestines, but there was a small, round head with huge eyes, undulating its way down the lower part of Max's large intestine. Stubby little tentacles allowed it to crawl forward. *Kohei.*

"He has your head," Max said.

"He possesses his own appendages," Rick responded.

Max honestly didn't know whether that was a translation failure or Rick's sense of humor. Sometimes it was difficult to tell. However, he broke out in near-hysterical giggles. He was a fucking officer and fighter pilot, but he couldn't seem to stop fucking giggling. Kohei looked like a little stuffed toy version of an octopus, but the sight of that bulbous little creature crawling its way toward freedom gave Max the strength to breathe through the pain and ignore his instincts.

The scanner caught the edge of another little tentacle, and Rick reduced the magnification. A second offspring wriggled much more quickly than his bulbous brother. And then he spotted the third one. It was half the size of the middle sibling, and it appeared to be swimming in the fluid around his medium-sized brother rather than crawling. That was not good. If it still had room to swim, it had to be tiny.

"Query. Can you stop the third offspring?" Max asked.

Rick's tentacles curled. "I cannot reach past Offspring One to touch Offspring Three. To save Offspring Three would require dismembering Offspring One."

Max closed his eyes and let his head thunk onto the cold exam table. Rick's tentacles offered comfort in the form of small strokes, which made Max feel even worse. Rick might lose a child. He shouldn't be the one offering comfort.

Max watched the children. Kohei was wriggling now, desperate to get free, and Max felt the strain in his entire body. If he hadn't been able to see Kohei, he wasn't sure he would have the strength to avoid pushing. Offspring Three swam like a jellyfish with all his tentacles flowing out before they all rushed back together again. He wasn't getting anywhere because he didn't have the room inside what appeared to be his brother's birth sac, but he was sure trying. His little tentacles kicked and twitched and curled, and Max felt sick to his stomach. "Query. Could small offspring survive being born now?"

"Unknown." For long minutes, Rick said nothing. Kohei's first few tentacles reached the exit ramp, and Rick pulled his tentacle out right before Max felt small slapping movements against his ass. "Survival requires a body large enough to maintain internal warmth and limbs strong enough to maintain movement. Nutrients are absorbed through movement in water," Rick said.

Max looked at the smallest offspring with those tentacles madly kicking, and he had to hope that Offspring Three could survive. Suddenly all the pain vanished. The sense of having a butt at all vanished. Half of Max's body disappeared.

"Offspring three has ejected the...." And Rick's sentence ended with a series of ear-splitting shrieks.

"Translation matrix failure," Max said.

Rick's tentacles uncorkscrewed a little. "Offspring eject hormone to relax host muscles. You may be gross after offspring appear, but birth will move quickly now."

"Wait, what?" Max propped himself up on one elbow. His body was still there. Thank God. But Max couldn't feel anything as a mini-Rick, smaller than a football, slipped free of his body. The stubby tentacles waved in the air and curled, but it was silent. Unlike his father, he lacked any red markings and his body was mottled gray and beige.

"Query. Is offspring healthy?" Max asked, slurring the words. His elbow slipped and he would have face-planted onto the table, but Rick's tentacles caught him and eased him down.

"Offspring One is healthy."

"Cute," Max mumbled. It was. Its eyes were huge, and sure there were too many, but that couldn't counteract the frilly mantle that wrapped around the bottom of his head or the stubby tentacles or the oversized head. It was absolutely adorable.

"Earth people are weird," Rick said, but then the world started fading away. Max dimly realized that word the translator had missed was some sort of general anesthesia. Max fell asleep as Rick was telling him something about Offspring Two.

Chapter Eleven

When Max woke, he was in his bed alcove in the tiny space he thought of as his bedroom. The thin sheet was tucked around him and any evidence of bodily fluids had been removed. Rick had been busy.

Max sat up and winced as his ass complained about the abuse it had suffered. He touched the puffy entrance. It was sore, but no worse than if he had overindulged in some vigorous sex while drunk. He never used enough lube when he was drunk.

Max swung his legs over the edge of the bed and cradled his head in his hands for a couple of minutes. He was strangely woozy, which he hoped was a simple case of hunger. He was thinner than he had been. It made sense that the children would create some sort of membrane around them and store up liquid, but for some reason, that hadn't occurred to Max. He had thought alien food had too many calories, and he'd been trying to run off the paunch he had developed.

For the first time in his life he had those Adonis creases over his hip bones all the male models had in gay magazines. Max had wondered if they only appeared through the magic of photo manipulation. Not even the gym rats on base had them.

Apparently a lot of running plus working out added to an alien pregnancy resulted in hot hips.

Max stood and grabbed the wall to keep his balance. His first stop needed to be for food. A lot of it. And after that, he needed to go find out what had happened to the children. That was a conversation Max was not looking forward to having.

If they had lost the third child—and given how small it was, Max assumed they had—Rick would be miserable. Max had no idea what he was supposed to say to a father who'd been forced to watch a child die. Aliens had all this advanced technology and spaceships and intergalactic drives, or at the very least, interstellar drives, but they couldn't save one premature baby.

Max wondered if that was some philosophical stand on medical intervention. Maybe aliens were Christian Scientologists. Or maybe Rick didn't have enough money to buy the right medical equipment. Maybe he had spent his last dollar hiring a surrogate.

The thought inspired the intense levels of guilt that usually required his mother and a major national holiday, but it made sense. It wasn't as if Rick had a lot of crew around to draw salaries, so whatever he did, maybe he didn't make enough to have underlings. And Max assumed medical equipment was expensive in any culture.

Max wandered to food storage and grabbed a couple of the bars that had an almost chocolatey black bean flavor to them. Those were not two foods Max would've put together, but the combination worked. It was better than the small round discs that tasted like someone had chemically joined an asparagus and a fart.

He had finished one bar on his way to the infirmary. Since Max had woken up naked, Rick must have left Max's clothing somewhere. Max normally swam in his underwear, so the swimming pool was the most likely place to find his pants and shirt; however, Max wasn't ready to deal with a grieving father yet. And since the children needed water, Rick was going to be there. As long as Max didn't track Rick down, he could hope the third offspring was alive. Once Rick told him the child had died, it would be real.

The exam room was empty, but a half dozen tools were scattered on the floor and table. Rick was usually meticulous about putting everything away, which made sense in an environment where an emergency could lead to zero gravity or unexpected acceleration that would turn objects into projectiles. Max gathered the tools off the floor and grimaced at the slime that had pooled around a few. It smelled like urine and had the viscosity of dog slobber. Using two fingers, Max carried them over to the cleaning unit. When he opened the drawer, he found his underwear.

A little grossed out at the alien wash-all, Max took his underwear out and put the medical equipment in the same drawer before securing it again.

With his underwear on, he felt a little less vulnerable, although he doubted he would feel normal anytime soon. Kohei had been incredibly cute, and now Max wondered if he would be welcome around the children he had given birth to. If Rick didn't want Max near his children, Max couldn't blame him. From Rick's point of view, Max was a strange alien from an unrecorded species. That was not an ideal situation for a nanny. Which was another reason why Max should have figured out the truth long before he had.

Walking toward the pool felt like a funeral march. Max hated himself for getting too fucking involved. He always led with his emotions, even when common sense warned him to avoid getting too invested in someone who didn't feel the same.

Max walked into the pool room with his stomach churning. He spotted Rick in the water. He had taken his hat off, something he didn't do unless he feared getting in a splash war. Before Max had introduced him to the concept of horseplay, Rick had always floated upright with his weird fisherman's type hat in place. Right now he was floating so low in the water that only a few of his eyes were visible above the surface.

Max spotted the rest of his clothing in the corner, but he ignored it for the moment. He edged closer to the water, stopping when he was ankle-deep. "Rick?"

Calling Rick's name caused three or four of his tentacles to flail and splash. Rick rotated, and Max spotted the first child. He was the size of a football but beige with a few streaks and spots of mint green. All the gray had vanished. He spun in mad little circles, and his tentacles waved faster and faster until his head resembled a top. Max was guessing that was Kohei. Either that or Rick had two insanely athletic gymnasts for children.

"Query. How are the offspring?" Max left the question generic so if Rick chose to avoid talking about the third child he could.

Rick floated toward him. "Offspring One," he said as he touched the whirling dervish of a baby octopus. He paused with his tentacles curled up under his body before resuming his wild athletics. He was going to be a handful. "Healthy and absorbing nutrients quickly," Rick said. A tentacle pointed toward a water filtration island. "Offspring Two healthy and absorbing nutrients quickly."

Max looked, and the second offspring had climbed halfway up the water purification pipe using his walking tentacle, which was only slightly less stubby than his other tentacles. This one had less green and more beige and white. While Max watched, he slipped, falling back into the water with a splash. Max took a step closer, half afraid the child had gotten hurt, but the little one pulled his smaller tentacles up tight against the underside of his body and swam away to explore the far end of the pool.

"Good." Max nodded and did not ask after the third child. His heart ached at the thought of that tiny creature swimming madly in his brother's birth sac. He had been so full of life. Max's eyes stung, and he brushed the back of his hand across them. "Good. I'm glad they're healthy. And I was right, they're cute."

Rick came into the shallows and braced his walking tentacle on the bottom before he tilted his body. Two of his tentacles parted to show a palm-sized octopus tucked up against the place where tentacles joined the bottom of his body. "Offspring Three is small."

Max's legs turned to jelly, and he couldn't support his own weight. He sat down so fast that water splashed up around him and Rick slid backwards into deeper waters. "Oh, thank God. He's alive." A few tears slipped free, and Max scooped water up and splashed his face. "Query. Is he healthy?" He was so damn small.

"He is growing." Rick pulled his son away from the bulk of his body and into the shallow water before uncurling his tentacle. The little one swam vigorously, all of his tentacles contracting in unison like a jellyfish.

"That's good, right?" Max asked.

Rick kept his tentacle near the child the whole time, and after a few minutes, those tiny stubs of tentacles started to slow. Rick wrapped his limb around the child and pulled it close again. "Must stay warm to stay healthy, but must move to gain nutrients to stay healthy."

Max watched Kohei. He had slowed and was now swimming in circles. Most of his tentacles were tucked up close to his belly. Immediately Max spotted the problem. The smallest child was so small that he couldn't move without kicking all of his tentacles, which meant there was a lot of exposed skin to get cold. "But if you stay with him, he'll grow, right? Query?"

Rick paused. "Yes." The news sounded good, but Rick's tentacles were far too squiggly for him to be happy. Max narrowed his eyes and studied Rick. He was sluggish. The pool currents shoved him from side to side, and a few of his eyes seemed dull.

"Query. How long was I asleep?"

"Clarification. Not sleep. Hormone to relax hosts is produced by offspring. My offspring waited too long. I regret."

That sounded like redirection. "Fine. Query. How long was I passed out cold from baby hormones?" Max suspected most of that wouldn't translate, but Rick already knew what he was asking.

Again, Rick hesitated to answer. "Sixteen hours."

Fuck. That explained why Max had felt groggy and dizzy when he'd gotten up.

"Have you been down here with the offspring the whole time?" Max asked.

"Yes."

"Query." This time Max paused, not sure how to ask this. However, he couldn't walk away before knowing the answer. "Query. How long can you continue to shelter the offspring?" Whatever life cycle Rick's people had, they were not aquatic as adults. Never once had Max walked in to find Rick already in the pool. Clearly, the pool was something Rick associated with offspring and surrogates, not something he enjoyed for himself. And when Max had first walked in, Rick had been startled. That was the sort of reaction Max expected from someone who was exhausted.

"Many hours yet. He may still swim." Rick's tentacles turned into curly fries.

Max heart raced. The offspring would survive if his father could forgo eating or sleeping until he grew large enough to swim on his own. That wasn't likely. However, Max wasn't about to let him die. He stood and waded deeper into the water. "Show me what I can do to help him," he demanded.

Rick rotated to consider Max out of a new set of eyes, and then rotated again and considered him out of the large one that he normally used. "I can continue several hours."

"I know you can. But I think that little one needs more than several hours to grow self-sufficient. Query. Am I wrong?"

Rick didn't answer.

"We need to work together and take turns," Max said firmly. "I finished eating and sleeping, so I can handle several hours before I will need to pee and get more food. If you sleep now, you'll be able to take over and give me a break later."

"Query. You would care for offspring?"

If a human had asked that, Max would have been insulted. He still felt a hard knot of disappointment that Rick thought so little of him, but he knew Rick didn't understand him. "Of course I will care for offspring. I wouldn't let any child die, ever. I would risk my life for any child. But that child came out of me. I've already been protecting him, and I will not stop protecting him until I know he is safe." Max closed the distance so he stood right beside Rick. "Besides, it's not like I'm offering to give up anything other than some sleep and some time sitting at a computer database trying to teach your damn ship how to speak English. Query. How can I help?"

Rick rotated, his tentacles barely moving in the water as he did a full three-sixty and considered Max out of each of his various eyes. Max waited, willing Rick to trust him with this. Max would never choose sleep or personal comfort over the life of the child. Never. But he didn't have the vocabulary to explain his moral compass to an alien.

And he suspected that Rick's spaceship-sized inferiority complex didn't help. Several times he had told Max how much other aliens disliked him. That wasn't easing the way. But with the little one's life on the line, the big moron would either agree to a co-parenting plan or Max would make him.

Chapter Twelve

"I think I'll call you Xander," Max told his little friend who clung to his hand. Offspring Three was so small that he could hold on to the base of Max's pinky or the base of his thumb; he wasn't large enough to stretch all the way across the palm from one to the other.

"I don't think you guys get Buffy the Vampire Slayer out here, but you seem like a Xander." That was stretching the truth a little, but he went on to explain. "The other people on the show all had powers, but Xander had this grip on life. It was like he never gave up." Max moved his hand a little faster, and the baby held on tightly. "No matter what got thrown at him, he kept plugging."

"Now I'm not saying he was the brightest member of the Scooby gang, because he wasn't. He once showed up for a fight with a vampire carrying a rock." Vampires weren't real, but if they were, showing up for a vampire fight with a rock seemed a little stupid, and the older Max got, the stupider that moment seemed. "However, Xander kept plugging and he never gave up on life, and he never gave up on his friends. That's what you have to do now."

Max slowed as he ran his hand through the water. Rick insisted that was all Xander needed. As long as Xander had the warmth of Max's hand and help moving through the water, everything else would eventually fix itself.

"You have to channel your inner Xander and not give up. And maybe things are hard right now, and maybe they'll be hard for a while, but I saw you on that scanner. I saw you swimming for all you were worth when you were behind your brother. You're not the sort to give up easily."

Max turned and tried to find Offspring Two. He didn't seem to have any sort of middle child inferiority complex. He was not one to stand on the edge of things—or in his case float—and wail Marsha Marsha Marsha. Nope. Rick's middle child was determined to explore the far reaches of the pool. At one point, he'd even tried crawling out.

If Max hadn't been busy with Xander, he would've gone after the idiot. Luckily, the idiot in question decided that he was not quite ready to live in the open air, and he got back into the pool. Max needed to come up with some explorer's or adventurer's name for Offspring Two. He knew there were plenty. Some human had been the first to get the bright idea to go to the North Pole or South Pole. Those would've been great names, only Max was far better with television characters than historical figures. So for now, the kid would stay Offspring Two.

"I bet I'm breaking about a million taboos by giving you nicknames," Max told Xander. The warmth of Xander's body against his palm was a comfort. "Before going overseas on my first assignment, we got this whole lecture about cultural sensitivity. They told us how some people would never encounter an American other than members of the service, so we had to become ambassadors of a sort." Max snorted. That had stressed him more than live weapons training.

"That's a lot of pressure for twenty-four-year-old kid. I signed up to fly airplanes not to be an ambassador. And then they told us how it was even more important for officers to be culturally sensitive. They explained that whatever we did, the enlisted would take it as a signal they could do something three times worse. So if we were to do something heinous, they would do something worse, and it would be our fault." Maybe Max was bored or maybe he liked having an audience who couldn't understand him, but he found hanging out with the kids cathartic.

"That was a lot of pressure, and I was glad I didn't get stationed somewhere isolated enough that my lack of cultural sensitivity would lead to some international incident. I'm pretty sure my officers were nervous about me being gay, because there are parts of the world where gay does not go over well. However, my point is that if my training officers saw me doing such a culturally inappropriate thing as naming somebody else's children," and at this, Max brought Xander close to the surface of the water and made puffy faces at him, "they would probably go back in time and flunk me. Funny thing though, I'm not entirely sure I'm going home. Ever. So I think I need to stop living my life like I will be. I'll stick around and name you, if you don't mind."

Max lowered himself until his mouth was underwater then blew bubbles at Xander. Several of Xander's tentacles waved, and then Xander pushed off from Max's hand and swam madly for Max's face. His stubby tentacles caught at Max's lips, and Max blew more bubbles. Xander's tentacles danced across Max's cheeks and up into his nose.

Max snorted and caught Xander in his hand. "Okay. No snotty tentacles for you, sir."

Xander wrapped his tentacles around Max's thumb and pressed his belly to Max's palm. In that short swim, he had already cooled significantly. "If your father told me that he was upset with me for giving you names, I would stop," Max said. "Of course I named your father after a belching cartoon character and he doesn't seem to mind. You have a pretty laid-back father, but he was still awfully worried about you."

Kohei swam up and caught Max by his left wrist. "What's the matter? Are you tired?" Max waved his arms as if he were jogging in slow motion. Kohei's grasp was viselike, especially when Max compared it to Xander's light grip.

"You're welcome to hitch a ride for a while," Max told Kohei. It wasn't like he was going anywhere, not with Xander needing him. "You get so crazy with your gymnastics that I'm hardly surprised you wore yourself out. You have to learn to pace yourself."

The doors opened, and Rick came in with his hat back in place. He looked better than he had. Considering he had been on the verge of exhaustion, it didn't require much to look better than half-dead. "Query. Did you manage to get some sleep?" Max asked.

Rick slid toward the pool. "I slept two-point-three-seven hours."

That was not helpful. "Query. What is considered a normal amount of sleep for your species?"

"Five-point-two hours."

So he hadn't slept long enough, but Max couldn't blame him. "Well at least you got some sleep. But both of us need to pace ourselves so that we don't get too tired. The kids need us both rested and fed. Query. Did you get some food?"

"Not yet. I shall." Rick came into the water until it was halfway up his walking tentacle. Max lifted his hand so that Rick could see Xander still cradled in his palm. "The offspring are fine, but I'm not giving them back to you until you've eaten. You need to be strong."

Rick came closer, his tentacles reaching out toward Max and the kids. "You have tended them long enough."

"I had a long sleep. I feel wonderful, so you need to take enough time off that you feel wonderful before you take over. All the children are fine. Offspring Two seems a little overconfident, but Offspring Three is fine and healthy."

"Query. Clarify overconfident." Rick rotated, and he only stopped once his largest eye was pointed at the far corner of the pool where Offspring Two was busily sticking a tentacle out of the water like a flag. When Max turned, Kohei launched himself toward his brother.

"Bold. Reckless. He crawled out of the water before deciding that was a bad idea," Max explained. At this point he was almost more worried about their little daredevil than he was about Xander. Daredevil. Huh. Matthew Michael Murdock was the original

Daredevil. Max wondered if that would be a good name for the wild child.

"Offspring must learn boundaries," Rick said. He turned back toward Max and reached a tentacle toward Xander.

"I agree. I just hope he doesn't break something before he figures out where those boundaries are." It was probably a good thing that Rick's people didn't have bones because the middle child would've already broken a couple. He was precocious for a one-day-old.

Rick ran a tentacle along Xander's back, and Xander reached for his father without letting go of Max's hand. Rick might have a warm body, but his tentacles were far too chilly to keep Xander healthy. That was why Rick had to hold his son close to his belly.

"Query. Are humans born with full cognitive abilities?" Rick asked.

Max snorted. "No. Not even close. Humans are born with the potential for intelligence, but we pretty much roll around, cry, and eat for the first several months." He frowned. "Actually, we can't even roll for the first few weeks. And then it takes years before real cognitive processing skills develop." Max had to assume Rick was trying to make a point, so he waited for Rick to continue.

"Query. How long is required between birth and attainment of cognitive processing skills?"

"Query. Clarification. Any cognitive processing skills or reasonably well-developed skills? Because those will have different answers."

Rick floated closer. "The people are born with cognitive skills, but they lack experience to contextualize knowledge or apply innate instinct to universe." He curled his tentacle so it surrounded Xander.

"Are you saying they're born smart? I mean, are they born able to understand cause and effect?" Max asked.

"Yes." Rick shifted his tentacle away from Xander and curled it around Max's wrist. The contact caught Max off guard. A flash of connection—of longing—made Max ache even more when Rick then used his tentacle to wave Max's hand through the water. Of course. He wanted to keep Xander fed and healthy.

Max tried to appreciate the break from the endless movement and his sore muscles, but the touch reminded him of a hard ache in his soul.

"It makes the people unfamiliar compared to other beings," Rick said, and Max realized that Rick was trying to explain his species as a whole. "Others believe in raising young, but our young only need protection in order to learn context and language."

Max studied Xander as he clung to Max's ring finger and pinky. No matter what Rick said, Max refused to think of Xander as anything other than a helpless child.

Rick didn't say anything else, and Max started feeling like he was letting his half of the conversation down. "Okay," he said.

Rick kept using his tentacle to propel Max's hand. "I wish to contextualize information on human preference."

"Query. What sort of preference?"

"Preference regarding entertainment."

Max hoped that Rick was about to ask about some inconsistency in the *Star Wars* movies. Max didn't remember the prequel as well as he should have, so he had no doubt that he'd screwed up any number of details. However, if this was about to turn sexual, Max would rather avoid inappropriate conversations, and that went double when children were present. It went triple when he needed time to patch a few rough spots on his own soul.

Rick gently reclaimed his smallest son, shifting Xander to the side. However, he continued to hold Max's wrist. The red-tipped end of Rick's tentacle even curled around Max's fingers in an alien version of holding hands that came too close to Max's feelings for comfort. No way did Rick understand that the sort of respect and care and patience Rick had shown would trip Max's trigger, and holding tentacles probably meant something like gratitude. Max just wished it didn't hit so close to what he wanted. If Rick had been a human male, Max would've climbed him like a tree. But he wasn't. He was a bit of a helicopter octopus who didn't understand human feelings and why it hurt to hold hands.

"Query. What prerequisites are required for the activation of the reproductive system?"

Shit. Max had hoped the conversation wouldn't go there. "Query. Why do you require this context?" he countered.

"I wish to understand why I activated the reproductive system the time I touched you for implanting of offspring."

Max closed his eyes. The universe hated him. It did. However, he didn't want to verbally strike out at a guy who had suffered a shitty week. "It's like I said. If I'm in pain, you can't activate the reproductive system because I won't enjoy it. I don't like being in pain."

"Avoidance of pain is a universal trait." Rick seemed remarkably sure of that, and Max chose not to strip him of his illusions. Avoiding pain was not universal. Sometimes it scared Max how many people liked trading a little pain with sex.

"Well then, you have your answer. The required prerequisite is lack of pain."

Rick didn't answer for some time, but he also didn't let go of Max's wrist. "Query. Is there no other prerequisite?"

"What you mean? That was a query, by the way."

"If a law enforcers from ship had put a tentacle inside your body, would that have activated your reproductive system?"

Max so wanted to avoid this. And if he couldn't, he wished he could treat the whole thing like a joke, but his words about being an ambassador echoed in his head and mocked him. He was an officer. He had an obligation not to fuck this up royally. That meant he had to choose his words carefully. "Hell no. I didn't understand what was going on, and those guys were rude. They yanked me out of my plane and then acted like I was unreasonable for requesting that they put me back where they found me."

"Query. Why would law enforcers remove you from your mode of transportation?"

"There was something about my plane being about to blow up."

Rick's tentacles all twitched, and the one holding Max's wrist jerked hard enough to pull Max through the water a short distance. Now he and Rick floated mere inches apart. "Query. You wished to return to the plane before it blew up?"

"No. But I wished to be in my plane and not have my plane blow up. I wished I was still on Earth. I wished many things, and the law enforcers were not good at explaining anything."

"Query. Clarification. Pain and confusion preclude the activation of reproductive system."

Max had never thought of it that way, but it was weirdly accurate. "Yes."

"Query. Are any other conditions required?"

Max sighed. He didn't normally reflect on feelings this much. Being gay meant he had the freedom to opt out of certain "manly" activities. Peer pressure had never convinced him to play football or engage in middle school games that had involved punching friends. However, Max was guilty of avoiding emotion. And when he didn't avoid it, he sucked at it. The military hadn't exactly discouraged the trait. "You're asking me a question I can't answer. Human beings are all different. Some people's reproductive systems turn on for different activities or in different circumstances. I can't give you an answer for why a human's reproductive system turns on."

"I do not ask about humans. I understand individuals are different within a species. I ask about you." Rick shifted so his tentacles floated around Max in a mock almost-hug. They brushed across Max's arms and back, and shivers ran up Max's spine.

"Are there other prerequisites for turning on the reproductive system of Max?" Rick asked.

Max focused on Xander curled around his father. When he was right up against Rick, the contrast in colors was more noticeable. Xander had no green at all. From the top of his head to the end of each tentacle, he was a creamy beige. Rick tightened the circle of his tentacles and increased the gentle touches. "Query. Why are you asking for the reasons my reproductive system turned on?"

"I require context. I do not understand Max Davis."

Max snorted. "Join the club."

"Query. Clarify club."

"Sex is not easy to explain. I dislike that my reproductive system turned on that first time. You should not have to deal with me spilling genetic material."

"Query. Would that be gross?"

Max laughed. "Yes. It was gross. And I am old enough that I should not be gross."

"Query. Does that imply you were in pain or confused when I examined you for implantation of offspring?"

Max pulled at his hand. Rick held on for a time before letting go. Max did a backstroke to retreat from the area, but Rick followed. When Max was near the water filtration island, Rick caught his ankle. Damn aliens and their ability to hang on to umpteen things at once. Max caught the edge of the filtration island, and Rick drifted close enough to hold Xander in the currents.

Rick floated a few feet away and withdrew his tentacles. "Query. Did I harm or confuse you?"

"No," Max answered quickly. He watched Kohei spinning closer.

"Query. Would you want reproductive entertainment again?"

"What?" Max spun around to stare at Rick with horror. "Why would you ask that?"

Rick floated and stared at Max so long that Max thought the lack of a "Query" marker in front of the question confused him, but then Rick said, "I am without context."

"For our sex? Simple, the computer mistranslated surrogate for nanny and you did things that caused my reproductive system to turn on." And that was the unsexiest description of tentacle sex Max could manage.

"Confirmation. You said humans enjoy sex."

"Yes," Max said, feeling a little like he was walking in a minefield.

"Clarify. Query. Why would you avoid sex if you enjoy it and I meet the prerequisite conditions?"

Max closed his eyes and leaned back. Lord help him. He was about to lose his mind trying to explain shit that should be repressed and forgotten. However, he wanted to avoid miscommunication. Besides, if Rick's people found their way to Earth, he didn't want them all offering sex based on Max's unhelpful descriptions.

"Sometimes sex is all about the body. When I'm only thinking about how body parts fit together, it's quite easy for my reproductive system to turn on. But that sort of sex doesn't get talked about."

"Query. Why would entertainment involve silence?"

Max opened his eyes and tried to figure out how he was supposed to explain shame and Puritan ideals and parents and guilt, and all the garbage that went along with "easy" sex. And then there was the more complicated issue of gay sex. Without pregnancy to worry about and with the free-love sixties still driving the youth culture, a whole generation of men had rejected the idea that they should feel shame, and the lack of birth control in a population that literally didn't have to worry about birth had contributed to the AIDS epidemic. Max had barebacked once, and the guilt had congealed into a hard, crusty edge on his conscience for months. And that was still better than some of the guys who insisted AIDS wasn't any big deal. They barebacked and never got tested and pretended the seventies and eighties never happened.

How could Max translate any of that into terms that would make sense for an alien? "Answer. I don't know," Max said. He expected

Rick to demand answers, but he floated next to Max with his tentacles hovering around Max. They were silent for a long time, and Kohei swam toward his brother who was, once again, experimenting with walking in the shallowest part of the pool.

"However, sometimes sex involves how bodies fit together and the emotions that people feel for one another. That sex becomes complicated, and turning on the reproductive system too quickly can be a problem." At least it had always been one for Max. His relationships fell into two categories—short, hot, and likely to die faster than an advent candle, or long, messy, and emotionally damaging. "Emotions are harder than allowing the body parts to line up."

"Query. Does that imply you feel emotions?"

Now the universe was mocking Max. "Yes."

"Query. Positive emotions or negative ones?"

Max sighed. If he were honest, he would say both. He liked that Rick listened and that he explained and he wanted to know about Max. He appreciated the care he used around Max. He respected Rick as a father and felt sympathy for the way he'd suffered. But he also had a big dose of fear that he was getting too involved and that Rick didn't understand how much he was asking of Max. He was fucking terrified that he relied on Rick too much, and he had no idea what would happen when the time came for them to separate. And under that, he didn't want to hurt Rick because Rick had made enough comments about the shittiness of the universe in general that Max recognized how fragile he was. And that last truth convinced Max to give the simple lie instead of a more complicated truth.

"Positive emotions, Rick. I feel positive emotions."

Rick floated near him, his tentacles barely moving to keep him from drifting off in the current.

"Now go get something to eat and take at least an hour or two to recover before coming back and giving me time to get some food." Max extricated Xander from his father's tentacles. Xander grabbed onto Max's fingers and held tight.

"Yes." Rick turned and swished all his tentacles the same way Xander did. It shot him across the pool and he hurried toward the exit.

Max looked down at the baby clinging to his hand. "What am I going to do with your father?" he asked sadly. The worst part was that he suspected Rick would take far fewer emotional hits than Max would, in the end. Well, he could only handle one day at a time. The rest would have to sort itself out.

Chapter Thirteen

"James," Max called, "spaceships are on display again."

From the far side of the pool, a beach-ball-sized object streaked through the water so fast that when he hit Xander, he sent Xander tumbling in the water. Bold and obsessed with spaceships—the name "James" fit when it came to Offspring Two.

In the past month, James had more than quadrupled in size and had become possessive of the underwater instructional display that Rick had set up. Rick streamed everything from nature videos to detailed instructions for the building of spaceships. Xander was obsessed with the nature documentaries.

Max had learned a lot about Rick's people.

They had huge buildings that jutted out of a green ocean. Their haphazard cities featured towers that rose straight up, but also ones that shot out at odd diagonals. It looked like a supersized version of the crazy crystal formations that Max's brother had grown for his fifth grade science class. Thick cables joined the tallest towers, creating one huge structure, and small cable cars would zip from one tower to another. Max liked those scenes, but James was all about the spaceships.

Hopefully, James wouldn't turn out to be quite as much of a man-whore as the character he was named after, not that Max had a problem with man-whores. In fact, he was rather fond of them in certain circumstances.

Max returned to his work on the portable computer station Rick had set up when Max refused to leave the offspring, not even after

Xander insisted he could swim alone. While Rick knew his species, Max knew he couldn't concentrate if the children were alone.

After all, every once in a while Xander would still call out that he was cold.

Max wanted to be there to get in the pool with him when that happened. Xander's brothers were not the best at cuddling for warmth. Kohei would for a short period of time, but that child was still as hyperactive as ever. After a few minutes of snuggling with Xander, he wanted to go find some open space where he could twirl and generally show off his ever-lengthening tentacles.

And James was even less likely to cuddle. That boy was an adrenaline junkie. He would be the first to leave the water full-time. According to Rick, none of them could live on land until they were large enough to develop a complete digestive system, but James was trying to push the timeline.

Kohei would explore the room for short periods, and Xander would come as far as Max's computer workstation where he would watch Max work on the translation program for a few minutes before retreating to the water, but James was already going where no offspring had gone before. No corner was safe from his tentacles, and Max dreaded the day he could reach the door controls. The little monster would be impossible to corral. That wouldn't worry Max too much, except that their skin could dry out and as long as they were in this insane growth period, that would lead to their skin splitting.

Luckily for Max, a video on spaceships, or any sort of engineering would command James's interest pretty darn quick.

It was as if they had gone from being infants to being annoying tweens in a matter of a few weeks. Well, James had. Kohei was more like a teenager with an eating disorder trying to dance off calories, and Xander was still his little boy. According to Earth biology, the more complex an animal was, the longer the length of its upbringing. Rick's people seem to break that rule. Rather spectacularly.

"Hey there buddy," Max said as Xander lurched out of the water and stumbled toward him. After shutting the translation computer off, Max reached down so Xander could wrap his tentacles around his wrist. Xander was still smaller than the other children, but he had grown significantly. Kohei and James were both beach-ball size, and Xander was a little less than half that, but his tentacles were nearly as long as his brothers'. It gave him a long, lean look compared to his brothers' rounder bodies. Max thought the two older ones were cuter now. Xander had entered a gawky growth spurt stage where none of his body parts were quite in proportion.

But he was still Max's boy. Max had been a weird, gawky kid himself. Xander stretched his tentacles toward the computer, and Max held him close enough that he could push buttons. He repeated the startup sequence Max used for a new session, although Max wasn't sure if that was intentional or if Xander was simply repeating what he'd seen Max do. "Will you grow up to be a translator?" Max asked.

"Translator," Xander replied. In English no less. The other two spoke Rick's language and Max had instructed the computer's translator voice to use different pitches so Max could tell who was speaking, but Xander was learning his own language and Max's.

"You should learn a more useful language," Max said.

"Max useful." Xander tightened his tentacles around Max's wrist.

Max opened his mouth and then closed it again. He would call Xander a manipulative little shit, but the kid was learning English too quickly for Max to take the risk. "Max is a pilot. I'm a fighter pilot. I fly jets and shoot down any enemy." Max brought Xander up to eye level, and Xander reached for Max's neck.

"Max translates." He shifted over to Max's shoulder and pressed his body against Max's head. He'd grown so much that he was about the same size.

Max sighed. These days he was far more of a translator than a pilot. Watching a few of the videos that featured pilot technology convinced

Max he could never take up his old profession. On those videos, pilots had eight or ten tentacles all working different instruments at once. Max was a few tentacles short. Back home, the computer assisted with much of the flight. "Yes, I do." And when the translation job was done and Xander had asked for his last cuddle, Max would have to figure out something else to do.

Rick would let him stay. Max knew that. If anything, Rick seemed a little awed by the idea that Max liked him, and boy didn't that say something about Rick's self-esteem. However, Max needed to work. Even as buying a ticket home became a less likely possibility, Max refused to sit on his ass and let Rick support him.

"Down!" Xander said.

"I tell you what, why don't we go swimming together?" Max asked.

"Yes. Max swim with brothers," Xander replied enthusiastically. He was more verbal in his own language, but he liked to use English. Max stood and started unbuttoning his shirt. Xander was holding onto his neck so tightly, Max had to tug to get the fabric out from under him.

Max dropped his clothes over his desk chair and headed for the pool in his underwear. James could have cared less. He was far too involved in a technical explanation for the internal function of some sort of engine. It was the sort of information that the engineers back home would have given their firstborn to access, but Max didn't understand enough about the basics of alien engineering to even understand what was happening on the screen as blue smoke worked its way through what looked like a series of soda straws.

He would far rather swim with the children than watch that. He sank into the water, and Xander separated so that he swam next to Max's head. "What did you learn today?" Max asked.

Rick had said the children needed time to discuss their new understandings of the world in order to solidify information. That was why his people had three to five children at a time. The oldest would become a mentor of sorts for the others. Rick had then pointed out that Max had taken over as the eldest brother in the group.

Max could handle being their big brother. There was no way Max would call Rick daddy, though. That would fuck with his head more than he could handle.

At least his sex drive had returned. Max could indulge in a few "bunk" moments. Unfortunately, his imagination kept returning to Rick and all those tentacles. Even reenacting his favorite porn with himself in the starring role was hit or miss these days.

Luckily, Rick understood that Max was too emotionally involved to share any sort of sexual entertainment with him. Max couldn't enjoy cheap sex with a man who he had seen grieve over the near death of his son, one who had driven himself into the ground trying to make sure Xander survived, and who was kind to an alien stranger. Cheap sex was for men he didn't plan to see again, and who could be pricks, for all he knew. Rick was too kind and too insecure for any of that. If Max had sex with Rick, he would fall madly and deeply in stupid. So Max's only hope lay in avoiding any sort of physical entanglements.

When Xander started to talk, Max was pulled out of his own musings, and he had to mentally rewind the conversation before remembering that he had asked what Xander had learned during his time on the video display.

"Pajekh children are born with three sets of genitals, and when they reach maturity, they can choose which two of the three to keep, and the third is reabsorbed into their body." Xander sounded freakily excited by the idea. Max suspected their little munchkin was odd.

"Oh. Well that's special." Sometimes aliens were just so damn alien. "Are Pajekh nice people?"

Xander shot ahead, dove underwater and then he bobbed back to the surface. "They are all kinds of different people. Nice and mean and smart and dumb. They build big spaceships. The moon of home planet could fit in the belly of their spaceship."

"That's impressive." Either Rick's people had a small moon, or the Pajekh built damn big ships. Either was possible. A series of strange *thunks* went through the ceiling above them. "Your daddy is working on something." Max told Xander. Kohei stopped swimming the figure eights around the two filtration islands and darted their way. Max held his hands out so that his arms formed a circle and Kohei swam right for it. He shot through the center before catching Max's arm with his tentacles. His whole body swung around three-sixty so that he was eye to eye with his little brother.

"Do human children choose gender?" Xander asked.

Well that was a loaded question. "Not most of them." Max paused to unwrap Kohei's tentacle from around his neck. "Some humans are born with a little bit of each of the two genders. Sometimes their parents pick for them and sometimes their parents leave all the parts there until they're old enough to pick for themselves."

Kohei wrapped a new tentacle around Max's neck and pulled so he floated right in front of Max's face. "How can parents pick for them? Individuals have autonomy over their own bodies."

And that was another field of landmines. To hell with needing a linguist, Max needed some sort of diplomat up here, or maybe a sociologist. He was not qualified to answer the children's questions. His brother had never been quite so annoying. He'd asked stupid and innocuous questions like why the sky was blue or why didn't airplanes fall down. Max could answer one of those two.

The pool room door opened, and Max swiveled to greet Rick, thrilled at having another adult to rescue him from overly inquisitive children. Instead two strange aliens slid in, both pointing what appeared to be weapons straight at Max.

"Surrender!" one cried. The computer translated its chittering voice, but Max didn't need any help translating the way the smaller one raised his weapon. Fuck.

Chapter Fourteen

The two invaders stood near the door. They were four or five feet tall with oddly square bellies and muscular tentacle legs at each of the four corners. They had orangish, pyramid shaped torsos, and rounded edges made them look more like carved pieces of abstract art than living creatures. Each had a pair of plate-sized eyes on either side of the "front" rounded edge. Below their eyes, they wore a wide, metallic belt with hooks and pouches.

A fringe of shorter tentacles hung along the bottom of the torso, and each alien pointed a triangle-shaped instrument at Max. Considering that Max could see down the length of a barrel, he was guessing that was a weapon. A big-ass weapon the aliens held in three tentacles.

The invaders shouted at Max, but only two words translated, "Come" followed shortly thereafter by "Death." Despite the lack of common vocabulary, Max understood their intentions. He raised his hands to show they were empty, and hoped that was a universal gesture. He did not want to die in his underwear in an alien pool.

Actually, he didn't want to die, period. The specific details of his death would be the shit cherry on the fuck sundae. "I'm coming." Max inched closer. He pulled Xander's tentacles away from his arm and tried to push him back.

The invaders chattered again, and this time the translator offered, "Bring" and "also."

"They're children," Max objected. "Offspring. They're not part of this." Max didn't point out that he wasn't part of it either, but if he got the assholes to leave the kids alone, he would put that in the victory column. He was just grateful that James was nowhere in sight. Never before had Max been so appreciative of that boy's habit of wandering.

"Bring" and "also" came out in another round of chittering. The translator then spit out the words "Never" and "children," which they reinforced by adding "Born adult."

Rick had insisted that the people's offspring were cognitively mature from birth, but Max could not call these three adults. They were too small and too fucking naïve to deal with armed assholes. "Offspring can't leave the water. Children water. Adults land," Max argued. Kohei tried to pull himself around to the front of Max, but Max pushed the boy behind him.

"All come or die." That came out clearly and with a minimum of untranslated chitter. Max was not in a position to fight. He had no weapons, no clothing, and no idea what sort of conflict Rick had gotten them into. Was this an alien species that Rick's species had gone to war against, or had they been boarded by the intergalactic police?

Max had no idea. Well, he had some idea. He liked to think that no version of a police force would execute children for refusing to come. That put these invaders on his enemies-to-exterminate list.

But he had no way to kill them right now, so his best bet for survival and the survival of the children lay in cooperating. The boys were still clinging to him, so Max waded into the shallows. Walking toward an armed alien while wearing nothing but wet underwear was not a comfortable feeling. Not even a little. "Let me get my clothing." Max pointed at the chair.

The short invader chittered.

"Clothing." Max crossed his arms across his shoulders and mimicked shivering. Sadly, he had been playing this translating game long enough that he knew which ideas were easiest to translate. "Humans require covers. Humans cold."

Maybe these invaders had some sort of sympathy, because one of them walked over to the chair and used a small dangling tentacle to grab the clothing. He pulled it up toward what would, on Rick, be his mouth and flipped them around as though searching them. Max didn't even have a knife, so after a few minutes, he dropped them. Before Max could retrieve them, the alien kicked the shirt and pants in Max's direction. The hem of the pants landed in the water.

"Warm," it told Max.

"Yeah. Gee, thanks." Hopefully aliens didn't understand sarcasm, but given how few words were getting through the translation matrix, Max figured he was safe. He pulled his pants on over his wet underwear. This would not be warm. But he had a bigger concern.

He could not let the children's skin dry. Split skin could lead to them bleeding out. But these invaders did not seem to care. So Max dunked his shirt in the pool before he slipped his arms through the sleeves. It took a little poking and prodding, but he finally convinced the children to shift onto his back, so that they were between him and the wet shirt.

That would give them some protection. Kohei's long tentacles came up and curled around Max's neck. When Max tried to button his shirt, he discovered his uniform shirt did not fit two children under it. He tied the shirt tails around his waist instead, which left him bare chested.

Warm spots pressed against Max's back as the children pressed close. The small Xander spot slipped down near Max's waist where the shirt was tied, but Kohei stayed close to Max's neck, his tentacles shivering. The two invaders watched him, their symmetrical eyes locked on him, which was good because James was behind them. James's tentacles quivered a bit as he stood in the crevice by the environmental control machine. "Stay," Max said. The two invaders looked at him, and the taller one said, "Come." Clearly he assumed Max had been talking to him.

Max had to keep their attention off the far corner. "I come. Offspring stay." The shorter invader stepped forward and raised his gun.

"All come," Max agreed.

The taller alien turned and walked out of the pool room, and Max followed. Max's skin was already turning to goose flesh. The children had warm torsos, just like their father, so Max's back and neck were warm, but cold water ran down the crack of his ass and made his pants stick to his legs. Max suspected his brain was focusing on that because he was trying to avoid thinking too much about the armed invader walking behind him. If he fired, that weapon would hit the boys first. Fear knotted his stomach.

The invaders led Max up toward a part of the ship that Max thought of as Rick's territory. Back when Max had first started exploring the ship, these doors had all been locked, and at one point, he had seen Rick coming out of one of them. Behind Rick, Max had spotted a complicated computer panel that was four or five times larger than the one Max used for his translations. He had mentally labeled this the control level and had not tried coming back.

The large invader stopped in front of a door and pressed a short tentacle to the panel beside it. The door slid apart, showing a fairly large group of computer panels hung on the seven walls. None of the other rooms were hexagons, and this room was larger than any space other than the pool. Max had to assume this was an important room. An eight-sided couch dominated the center of the room and a large glass column rose from the center of that couch. The glass contained lightning, sparks that flowed from one pin-sized bit of metal embedded in the glass to the next.

Rick stood near the couch, so pale that his green appeared gray, and his tentacles were all curled into miserable little balls. Someone had thrown his hat into the corner, and Max knew the someone in question was not Rick. That man loved his tool hat.

"Rick, are you okay?" Max asked. He moved toward Rick, but an invader caught Max's arm.

"Max!" Rick's voice was unnaturally loud and belchy. "Query. Offspring?"

Max touched the tentacle still wrapped around his neck. "Kohei and Xander are right here. They're fine, and I'm doing my best to keep them wet."

The invader spoke so quickly that it was all one long chirping sound. The translator picked up a few random words including "work" and "die" and "offspring" and "aubergine."

Aubergine. Max had programmed that word himself, but he could not figure out why an alien would be using it, and he didn't like the implication of the other words the invaders were using. The flunky who had grabbed Max let go and backed toward his boss, but Max stayed put. He had to defuse the situation, but the problem was that he didn't understand it.

"Human. I offer compensation for surrogate care. Offspring," Rick said with a few extra belches standing in for words Max had not yet provided an English translation for. Unsurprisingly, Max had not covered hostage situations in his translation work.

Something in the translation matrix changed because coherent statements came out of the translator as the invader leader chittered. "Complete work or offspring die."

Rick quivered. "Conditional. I complete work. You kill offspring. Kill Max. Kill me." That was a little more direct and confrontational than Max would have preferred, but he couldn't fault Rick's logic.

"Conditional," the boss countered him. "You fail work. I torture offspring. I torture Max. I kill you."

As choices went, that did not sound promising. The threat made Rick shrink down on himself so that he was no taller than the invaders.

Max had never seen Rick's leg tentacle curl in stress, not even when they had thought Xander might die. But right now it was wavy and quivering. This situation was about to go from a hostage negotiation to a fucking bloodbath.

"Rick." Max said the name loud enough to demand Rick's attention. Rick quivered more. "Do the work," Max said firmly. The first rule of capture was to avoid death. Well, the first rule was to be prepared to give one's life in defense of country and the second rule was to continue to fight as long as one had the means to resist. However, the third rule for prisoners of war was to make every effort to escape, and escape required them to avoid catching a case of sudden death.

"Intelligent," the leader offered. Max didn't give a shit what that asshole thought. Anyone willing to kill children in order to extort someone and exploit their terror deserved to die, and Max would love to be the one to make that happen.

Chapter Fifteen

The leader alien stayed with Rick, and Max inherited one of the flunkies, who shooed him into the hall with a waving of tentacles and a few decisive air jabs of the triangular gun. One of the edges of the pyramid shape appeared to be the alien's front, based on its eyes being on either side of that particular ridgeline, and he held the gun on the left side of that center line.

Max had no idea how that helped, but he did try to stay closer to the right side of the alien, since the invader would have to shoot around his own body. His fringe of tool tentacles was shorter than the four leg tentacles, so he might hesitate to shoot across his own edge... nose... protuberance. It appeared an illogical body design.

"Go," the asshole ordered, with a leg wave to the left when they reached the first intersection. Max didn't argue because this little shit didn't have the power to negotiate. The boss had stayed with Rick, but Max had no way to help him. Hopefully, they would leave if Rick cooperated, but Max wasn't counting on that. He was counting on these guys putting him in a room with Rick. Then he could get more information and start planning.

The flunky ordered Max into a lift. The lifts were designed for one person, so Max had a moment of irrational hope that the guard would send him down before following. Max had explored every bit of the ship outside the command level, so he only needed a few minutes to lose himself in the labyrinth. The alien squeezed into the cramped space, his damn gun pressing into Max's stomach. Max braced himself against the corner walls and refused to give the asshole any more space. Rick might insist the offspring were tough, but Max would not lean against them, not when his damn shirt was already drying.

"You're safe, Xander. You're good, Kohei," Max said, but he kept eye contact with the alien. If these assholes saw the offspring as children, maybe they would be more inclined to show mercy. "Don't worry, kids. I'll protect you."

"Cold," Xander said in a small voice.

That was odd because his hot body was pressed up against the small of Max's back, but then Max realized they would swim together when Xander said that. Xander was so small, he was probably getting dry faster.

The tentacles around Max's neck loosened, and Kohei slid down Max's back so he was huddled around his brother.

"They're scared and cold and dry," Max said to the invader, and he hoped at least a couple of those words translated. He wasn't sure if the improved translation was a function of being in the control room or if the computer had aligned the languages, but he needed these guys to understand the danger.

The lift door opened, and the alien backed out before issuing a curt, "Come."

Max sighed, but after a few seconds, he followed the order. Max spotted two more aliens near the corridor that led to the medical room. That made five aliens so far, and Max didn't know how many he hadn't seen. The odds were not good, which was why he was still trying to play nice.

The guard kicked Max to get him to take the right turn at the next intersection. Max stopped. He turned and looked at the flunky. "Wrong direction."

The invader jerked toward Max as if he might head-butt him, or at least chest bump him. He wasn't the tallest alien in the world. "Move." He then raised his weapon.

Max clenched his teeth. This was absolutely the wrong direction. This part of the ship had claustrophobic cubbies or bunks that Max assumed were either used for fragile cargo or low-paid workers. It might be a seedy version of an alien barracks. But none of these cubbies had access to water. Without water, the children wouldn't survive long. Even James, as adventurous as he was, never stayed out of the pool for more than thirty minutes, and they were already coming up on that deadline. Max's wet shirt would not protect them for long.

"Offspring need water. Pool. Fluid." Max tried every synonym he knew in the hopes that something would get through to his captor. Tentacles tightened around Max's waist, and Xander started a steady stream of burps that came out so soft that the translator didn't pick them up. He knew something was wrong; Max was starting to regret that Xander knew so much English.

"Move."

"Offspring." Max planted his feet, but the next thing he knew, the flunky had struck out with one of his leg tentacles, kicking Max low in the abdomen.

Max collapsed to the ground, landing on his hands and knees. The blow had driven the air from him, and he gasped and retched as the pain ripped through him. Xander's belches turned into something louder and wilder, and infinitely more distressed, but Max couldn't focus on that. If this asshole locked them in one of those bunks, Max would have to watch the children suffer and bleed and die in his arms. The only reason Max was cooperating was to save the children, so if he had to choose another path to give them even a small chance of survival, he was okay with that.

"Move," the alien repeated. He didn't even bother raising his gun, but then again, Max figured writhing in pain undermined any machismo he might have had going for him, not that Max was a Rambo to start with. And he knew from Rick that aliens thought the human form looked frail and a little unbalanced.

After crawling to the wall, Max rested his hand against it a moment before he started climbing back to his feet. Fuck, he hurt. If that asshole had caused internal damage, Max's timeline would be even shorter. If he was bleeding internally, he had a limited amount of time to deal with this before his own injuries would make that impossible.

Max started heading down the corridor in the direction the flunky had indicated. The whole time, he kept his hands against the wall to steady himself. He stumbled several times, falling to his knees as he clung to the rail that lined most of these corridors. But each time, before the invader could strike out again, Max pulled himself to his feet and continued. Max had never been particularly religious, but now he prayed. He prayed to God or the universe or karma or whatever force controlled luck, because he needed to get to the next juncture.

If the invader was going to lock them into one of the nearest cubbies, Max would need to make a desperate move. But if he could get to the junction with the next corridor, he had options. Max continued to stumble along. Under his shirt, tentacles twitched against his skin, and Max had never felt so desperate in all his life. Even during that near-fatal training exercise, he had never felt such cold, raw terror. Back then, the only thing he faced was his own death, and now he had more to lose.

With each step, Max felt the tiny ember of hope grow brighter. As they approached the corridor that intersected their own, Max stumbled again, and fell to the floor. The guard didn't even react, most likely distracted by Max's feigned clumsiness.

He was taking a page from Xander, the original Xander. That Xander had shown up for a fight with a master vampire, rock in hand. Max could damn well show up to a gunfight with a maintenance rod. He wrapped his fingers around the rod-shaped hook tool hidden where the floor and wall met, and when he started to get up, the flunky moved closer to prod him into action.

Max spun around and darted forward. He aimed between the center leg tentacle that faced him and the one to the right, and he shoved that hooked rod straight up into the diamond shaped underside. The gun clattered to the lightly-padded decking, but Max ignored the temptation. He didn't know alien weaponry well enough to turn it against the invader, and Max needed to end this before reinforcements could arrive.

The rod sunk into the alien's flesh two or three inches, and the creature gave a high-pitched scream as its small tentacles all curled inwards, grabbing for that rod. Warm suction cups slapped against Max's arms and hands before wrapping around him.

Max suspected that a few inches of rod wouldn't prove fatal, so he shoved up with all his might. He drove it deeper into the invader's body. Then he yanked down. Hard. The hook, designed to pull up plating, ripped through something vital. Max smelled the stench of rotten eggs as greenish yellow bile flowed over his hands.

Not willing to risk an enemy at his back, Max impaled the guard again, and his hands sunk into the torn underside. Flesh squished, and Max knew this would feature in his nightmares later, but right now he had an obligation to protect his children. The flunky's screams turned into a wet gurgle. Death sounded the same in any creature.

Unwilling to prolong anyone's pain, Max wanted to end it. He ripped the rod out again. The invader's tentacles slowly uncurled as he sank to the floor. With one final surge, Max drove the hooked end deep into the alien body, this time right through one large plate-shaped eye. Sensory organs had to connect to a brain structure, and that must be the same for aliens because the body collapsed like an underinflated balloon.

Max felt squirming little ones at his back struggling to work their way up. One of Kohei's tentacles reached around to the front of Max's unbuttoned shirt, and the top of his head appeared.

"No," Max said as he held the fabric against his skin with blood-stained hands. "You don't need to see this." He quickly backed away from the body, but he couldn't lose too much time in an attempt to shield the children. He had to clean his hands off so he could climb and grasp tools and find water.

Those were on his short list of tasks to accomplish. His full list included slaughtering all the assholes who threatened his ship.

Chapter Sixteen

Max needed to get to water fast. He doubled back and headed for the nearest crew room. "Let's get you guys wet, and then we'll get back to the pool room."

The clock was working against them. The second an enemy found that body, they would all go on high alert. Any advantage Max had would be lost. However, he had taken the risk in order to save the children, so letting them dry out was not an option.

He rushed to the nearest crew quarters. "Let's get you wet. Kohei, hold your brother."

As he started untying the bottom of his shirt, he felt the boys shifting around at his back. There was a small service area under the pool room that had an open tank to feed the water filtration towers. The water ran too fast for comfort and Max worried that a stray tentacle could get sucked into the filter system, but that might be the safest place to hide the children. Once the invaders realized that Max was on the run, they would look in the pool.

Max toyed with the idea of leaving them in crew quarters with access to a sink, but he didn't like their odds of they were trapped in such a small space. At least in the filter room, mechanical pieces created niches and hiding spaces. And as James had already proven, the children knew how to hide.

Max slowly slipped the shirt off. The children clung to him, or Kohei did anyway, and he had a firm grip on his little brother. Max pulled the two offspring around. Sure enough, it was dry. Kohei wrapped his tentacle around the edge of the sink where Max had turned the water on, and he pulled himself and his brother up to the rim.

Xander was disturbingly pale, so Max scooped water over Xander before doing the same for Kohei. They were slopping water everywhere, but Max didn't care. He didn't even care if they left a trail for the invaders. He would care about that when they left the pool room. Once they got James, then Max could not risk having their movements tracked.

"Xander, query. Good?"

"No." Xander said, and it was the most heartbreaking syllable Max had ever heard.

"Okay, let's get you to the water. Let's get to James." Max lifted the boys onto his back before he rinsed the worst of the blood out of his shirt.

Xander made low belching noise that the translator completely missed. But Max had to put Xander's distress out of his mind and focus on the mission.

If he did not clear the area of enemy, all of them were in mortal danger. The same adrenaline that had driven him when he'd leapt into his jet as the sirens had gone off on the tarmac drove him now. He tied the two shirt arms around his neck to create a sling and tugged on Kohei's tentacles to urge him down into the sling. Then grabbed his weapons. He didn't even know how to fire the alien gun, but once he got the children to a safe place, he'd figure it out. These assholes would regret invading his ship.

Then Max would figure out what the fuck Rick was doing with his security that they could wander around the ship without any alarms going off. Max was starting to think that Rick had a few screws loose in the old head sack.

Max checked the corridor before he dashed for the lift. The lift would be the most dangerous part of this. If the doors opened onto a pair of aliens, he would have almost no ability to defend himself. He was confident he could take at least one with a good solid hook to the bottom of their body mass. Now that he had killed one that way, he knew how much force it would take to pierce that skin and do a lot of internal damage.

But that would give the second one time to counterattack. But, if Max tried to use the service corridor doors that he had found during his explorations, it might take too long. He would have to make more stops to keep the children wet and that gave the enemy far too much time to find their fallen comrade.

Max tucked the alien gun into his waistband and prayed that the thing had a safety. He needed both hands to grip the maintenance hook. He forced himself to breathe and steadied his nerves as the lift doors opened on the pool level. Empty corridor. "Thank God," he whispered. And then he ran as quietly as he could for the pool room.

The pool took up most of this level, so the invaders should have dismissed it from their minds as soon as they believed they had everyone captured. Aliens might have had great technology, but they couldn't tactically think their way out of a wet paper bag. He planned to take full advantage of that blind spot.

The pool room was dark when he went in, the illumination set to half power. "James?" Max let the door slide shut behind him, and he inched into the room. He was met with an anxious round of blurbles and burps and whale song.

"Max. You returned. Query brothers? Max. Query Rick? Query..." The translator failed, leaving ugly burping. Either James was practicing profanity or that was the name of their invaders. Max spotted James on the edge of the pool, his tentacles all curled up under him. Max hurried to the edge and let the shirt sling down into the water so that Xander and Kohei could soak themselves.

"You're going downstairs to the small pool room. I will find Rick," Max said.

All James's tentacles waved madly. "Max. Danger." James added a warbling cry the translator missed. He had a whole new set of experiences to program into the damn thing, just as soon as Max finished killing all the motherfuckers.

Xander countered with a long string of whale song that the translator was inadequate to handle. Out of the entire soliloquy, the translator only picked up "Max," "Rick," "maintenance hook," and "wet." However, with those clues, Max had a pretty good idea of what Xander was explaining. He was just glad the children hadn't seen the killing. It was bad enough they had heard it. If they didn't need therapy, Max would for exposing children to that kind of shit. The one thing he had always hated about shows like The Tomorrow People and Buffy the Vampire Slayer was how children were pushed into a fight that they were far too young to understand or emotionally cope with.

Max didn't care what Rick said about them being adults, they weren't. They might have the cognitive abilities of an adult, but they did not have the wealth of experience. A strong foundation in love and honor added to a long history of family support would help blunt the sharp edges of death. The children didn't have that yet.

Max went to his knees next to the pool. "Come on, we need to run." None of the children argued, and Max gathered them up and slipped them back into his sling after he'd wrung it out a little bit. Now was the time they couldn't afford to drip or leave any sign of their passage. The easiest way for these invaders to win was for them to find the children and use them as hostages. That made hiding them priority number one in Max's book.

He chose the exit that led to the mechanical workings of the ship instead of risking the lift. There was a narrow passage here, one Max had carefully shimmied down when he'd explored this level. At the time he'd hoped to find any cure for boredom as he waited for the mysterious children he was supposed to nanny. Now he slid down the shaft, slowing himself enough that he could control the six-foot drop to the floor at the next level. Max suspected the shaft had something to do with overflow of from the pool because it led into the lower filter room.

The light dribbled in from above where the filtration pipes led to the upper pool. It gave the room an ominous glow as that light bounced off the waves. Max walked to the edge of the pool, but he held on to the sling tightly. "Kohei, hold Xander. Protect Xander from moving water," Max said. Kohei was the most athletic, and Rick had said the eldest had a certain instinct to care for younger siblings. Max had to trust him to take care of Xander now, because Xander was not a strong enough swimmer to fight the current.

Kohei wrapped two tentacles around a pipe and held his brother with the rest. His tentacles and Xander's tangled together until they were one knot of octopus. "James, if enemy comes, hide your brothers. Show how to hide." Hopefully, he would find some good hiding spots in the room.

James curled his tentacles around Max's wrist. "I continue with Max."

"Absolutely not. No. You stay here with your brothers." Max tried to pull James's tentacles away, but he had more strength than Max had anticipated.

"I go Max. I know ship. I know access codes and internal scanners."

Max cringed because James did have a point there. If Max could use internal scanners to identify where the enemies were, his odds of success went up. But that did not justify putting James in the middle of a damn counterattack. "No. Show me how to access scanners."

"Too complex. Time too short. Must win enemy." For someone with a limited understanding of English, James was good at choosing words that would translate in order to communicate his ideas.

"No. Dangerous."

"All danger." James wrapped two more tentacles around Max's arm. "Quickly win enemy. I work scanners."

Max's hands started to lose some feeling. Fear and dread built in the pit of his stomach. They did not have time to fight about this because the enemy could find that body at any moment. Max lived in constant terror of hearing some alarm over the ship's systems. Of course, that was assuming that the ship had alarm systems because at this point, it didn't seem like anyone had considered internal security during its design. "I must go," he said firmly.

"I must go also."

Xander chimed in. "Max and James work against enemy together. Let James help."

Max glared at the obnoxious little traitor. Any other time he would have argued, but he couldn't waste another second. "Kohei, take care of your brother."

With one last look toward the two of them huddled together, Max took off for the door. "Query, where's the nearest console?"

James reached toward the wall, and Max checked both directions before he stopped near a glass panel. He had suspected they were control panels like on the translation computer, but nothing he did activated them.

James's motions were sure and quick as he called up an internal schematic of the ship. What Max had thought was a command deck was a transition of some sort between what appeared to be the lower decks and some sort of higher-security upper deck structure. With a few quick taps, James changed the display, and a number of dots moved around the various sections.

Two yellow dots were in the filtration room, and Max pointed at the display. "Hide them," he said.

James jerked his tentacles back. "Can't. Can only distract display."

Even though Max didn't understand what that meant, he dropped the issue. If James couldn't accomplish some piece of programming, Max wasn't going to guilt him about it. So he focused on his job. In the corridor outside the filtration room, one yellow and one blue dot blinked. That implied the computer was tracking different species rather than intruders and people who should be on the ship. Two dots were in the corridor by the medical room and two were outside the lower storage decks. The cavernous rooms were empty.

That was four more enemy in addition to the leader. One yellow and one bluish-green dot were still in the "control" room.

The medical corridor was the closest, so that was Max's first stop. Time to figure out the weapon. He urged James to move, so James curled his strong walking tentacle around his neck as Max dashed for the service shaft.

With every step, he expected to hear an alien voice shout or a weapon discharge or an alarm sound. So far the invaders were as tactically oblivious as Rick. Once he was far enough away from the filtration room that any noise he made would draw invaders away from the children, Max pulled out the triangular weapon and studied the short part of the triangle where the aliens had held it.

It had long grooves, and Max ran his finger along the indentations. He felt the slightest seam. He pointed the weapon away from the filtration room and pressed it. Nothing happened.

All the work on the translation computer had taught Max to seek creative work-arounds, so he switched to using his thumbnail. He ran a finger forward over the seam and then backward. He feared the weapon had a security lock, but then he drew a circle over the seam. The last-ditch effort paid off when energy gathered along the sides of the triangle and then discharged with enough energy to send the deck plates exploding up into the air before they clattered back to the floor in a twisted heap of rubble.

"Win," James said. He waved two long, slender tentacles.

James might be right. They might win. However, Max had to keep in mind that the other side had the same weapons, so Max had to play this smart. Time to move fast.

Chapter Seventeen

There was so much tactical information that Max wished he could ask for. However, he had never programmed certain words into the translator. He would frustrate James if he asked whether the weapon he had scavenged could breach the ship's hull. Max could only try to avoid weapons fire unless necessary, and then make sure that the energy hit the invaders and not the ship. Or at least not to hit the ship again. He hoped Rick would forgive him for the mess he'd made out of the decking.

Max stopped by one of the access vents set high into the wall and used the indented handhold to lift himself high enough to pry the cover off. He had done this dozens of times when he'd been exploring, but never with little tentacles in the way.

"Careful with tentacles," Max said.

"Careful with enemy," James replied. Either James had a wicked sense of humor or the translator was glitchy. It was a little hard to know which. Max gave James a little push to get him to slide back farther so he wouldn't interfere with arm movements. James shifted. That allowed Max to haul himself up into the service shaft before he started shimmying down to the level below.

He had hoped that he would be able to locate the enemy from within the shaft, but he couldn't hear anyone. For a time, Max considered doubling back and having James check the internal scanners again, but they didn't have time. Then in a wild tangent, his brain conjured an image of an ex-boyfriend.

At one point he'd had a brief but torrid affair with a man who wrote children's books. Bobby had always said he loved that for children, cliché didn't exist. An author could have the most clichéd, stereotypical villain, yet children would soak it all up because it was new to them. At the time, Max had thought that Bobby was a little too cynical to write children's literature.

But Bobby's words haunted Max as crawled back up the vent shaft.

"Max win enemy, query?" James asked.

"Watch and learn, young padawan. Watch and learn." Max had snagged several small chunks of metal from the exploded decking, and now he took the two smallest and dropped them down the shaft. He ran like a demon for the next shaft. This trick was so old that even cartoons considered it too clichéd to work. This was Wile E. Coyote territory. Max levered himself back up into the next ventilation shaft and shimmied his way down a level.

Sure enough, the chattering of agitated guards filled the air. Max found a horizontal shaft intersecting his original one to rest and reposition himself so that he could get his head down and peek through the grate. The two invaders were coming back down the corridor. One had a piece of metal clutched in a small fringe tentacle, and they chittered at each other without looking around. Hopefully they were stupid enough to investigate without reporting anything by radio.

Max slid out of the horizontal space. His shoulders ached from the awkward position in the narrow vertical shaft. It required him to brace himself like freaking Spider-Man, and James made that even more awkward by resting his weight against Max's head. A few extra shoulder muscles would have come in handy, but Max was Air Force. He went out of his way to avoid the sort of PT the masochistic Marines indulged in.

Despite his body's complaints, Max worked his way back up to another horizontal shaft and sat on the edge of it, watching the ventilation grate below him. He knew from experience that if he landed on the grate, it would open cleanly and let him drop to the floor below. He knew that, but he suspected that any alien walking under the grate might be a little surprised to find a human falling out of thin air. At least that was the plan.

The chittering came closer and Max braced himself on the sides of the shaft. At the same time, James tightened his leg tentacle a little too much. Max tapped the tentacle, and James loosened it immediately.

Then the two invaders walked under the ventilation shaft. Max pulled the maintenance hook out of his waistband and dropped down. His feet slammed the grate open with a reverberating metallic clang. Before the first invader even turned, Max lunged forward and drove the maintenance hook up into the invader's underbelly.

The enemy gave a chattering cry, and then screamed like a cat in heat. When Max tried to rip the hook back out, it caught on something. Rather than struggle with injured alien number one, Max abandoned his first weapon and turned to deal with the second invader.

The alien might not have anticipated an attack, but it was already moving fast. Alien two had his triangle weapon halfway out of what appeared to be a holster. Max pulled his own weapon and circled his thumb on the trigger even as the other alien was scuttling backwards.

Energy burst from the gun and slammed into the alien so hard that its body split above its wide disco belt. A fraction of a second later, the heat of the energy backwash blasted Max. He flinched away, raising his hands to protect his face and James. Burnt hair smell and the sensation of a cold breeze across his hands suggested Max had gotten burned badly.

When Max opened his eyes, the back of his hands and arms were lobster-red. The skin was damaged, but it appeared to be either a severe first-degree or mild second-degree. In an ideal world, Max would've gone to find something to cool the flesh. However, that was not possible.

"Query, James, healthy?" Max asked as he turned back to alien number one, the alien who didn't have his guts blasted across the corridor.

"Heathy, healthy," James said.

Then he was doing better than alien number one. The impaled invader was making soft chirping noises of distress, or at least Max assumed it was distress. But any sympathy vanished when it reached toward the dropped weapon. Not willing to risk another close encounter with an energy discharge, Max grabbed the bottom of the maintenance hook and yanked.

The hook came free with a whoosh of fluids, and the alien slowly sank to the floor. When its head began to indent like a sinkhole, Max grabbed the second alien gun and fled the scene. As he ran, he tucked both triangle weapons into his waistband, but he dropped the maintenance hook because it was too slick with the viscera for him to risk using it again. He'd have to grab another.

"Max hurts." James said with an unhappy burp.

"Enemy hurt more," Max replied. He wished he had the vocabulary to comfort James or explain the situation, but he didn't. They reached a ventilation shaft, and Max climbed up to grab the edge and pop it open. As he was scrambling into the narrow space, he hit his arm on the edge of the opening.

"God damn mother fucking son of a mother-fucking bitch!" The pain nearly made him fall back out, but he gripped the cover with one hand and the edge of the latching mechanism with the other. After a couple of breaths, he pulled himself up into the shaft and started climbing to the nearest horizontal shaft.

"That is why you do not use unfamiliar weapons," Max whispered as he crawled. He didn't think that he could pull that trick off again, not when climbing required him to brace himself with his arms.

With every enemy he took out, he took more damage to himself. If these aliens had reinforcements on a ship nearby, he was so very screwed. Max wasn't some bad-ass Ranger. He wasn't even a Marine. He was a fucking zoomie. He wasn't supposed to be the one engaging in hand-to-hand combat with alien invaders.

"Max hurts," James said again, this time without any additional burps.

"Max hurts," he agreed. There just wasn't anything he could do about it. He needed to make a pit stop to get James wet, and he needed to kill the rest of the invaders before his injuries could slow him down too much. "Where is the next console? We need to check for enemy." The idea of having to fight again made Max teeter between feeling homicidal and despairing.

James pointed up with a free tentacle, and Max wanted to groan. He had to climb again. Never one to postpone the inevitable, especially when postponement would give the injured tissue more time to swell and cause more pain, Max started climbing.

A quick check on the computer revealed that the next two aliens were still near the empty storage hold. If Max could get them both to stand in front of the doors and open them, he could shoot them from the far side of the hold, but he didn't know the weapon's accuracy. Worse, if he missed, he would have precious few options for cover in that area of the ship.

James touched one end of the hall. "I take weapon here."

For a second, his horror was so intense that Max couldn't find words. He wanted to scream and rail, but he knew how the children reacted to any suggestion that they needed help, particularly James. He was the most contrary, self-reliant, stubborn little octopus in creation. "I don't want you to kill."

"Query. Reason." James sounded offended. Maybe Max was projecting because the translator's voices didn't seem to convey tone.

"You are young. I don't want the young to kill." Max wished he could explain better because the end of James's tentacles were curling in frustration. Xander had done that a lot when he'd been too young to follow his brothers around the pool.

"I am cognitively mature."

"You are young and you have not had many experiences. You should not have to remember killing."

"You killed."

The words were so simple, but Max felt them like a fist. He had killed. He'd shot down an enemy plane back when he'd been stationed in the Middle East for a few months, and now he'd used his hand-to-hand training to take the lives of three aliens who had as much right to live as any other sentient creature. Max didn't regret his actions, but he regretted that he'd been forced to take them. He knew that fine line would cost him a lot of sleep in the near future.

"I have more experiences with life, with protecting life and loving people. That makes the pain a little less."

"Pain? Query. Physical pain?"

Right now Max was in physical pain and relying on adrenaline to control the worst of it, so he didn't have time for this conversation, but James would do something stupid if Max couldn't convince him to stay out of the fight. "No. Pain in the soul, in the emotions. All life has value, and ending a life means ending that value."

"Clarify. They would kill you." Maybe James assumed Max was too stupid to understand that.

"Yes. That is why I kill them. I will not allow them to kill either of us. But I don't want you to kill. You need time to learn to value life before taking it."

James tightened his leg tentacle around Max's neck before loosening it again. Maybe he understood. Max decided to push his luck. If he had to take a big risk, he wanted James safe. Max pointed to the map. "Stay here. Wait."

Max knew he was in trouble the minute James's tentacles curled. "No. I go with Max. Max not alone."

"I move faster alone. I don't have to worry about hitting you or you holding too tight," Max explained.

"I hold loosely. I go with Max." Despite his words, he tightened his leg tentacle.

"I move more quickly if I'm not worrying about you. I need you safe. Wait here." Max touched a guest room on the opposite side of the ship from the storage space where the two remaining aliens were standing guard. It wasn't the best solution in the world since Max still didn't know how the aliens had gotten onto the ship or whether they had reinforcements ready to board. He was flying in the dark, and unlike when he literally flew in the dark with his fighter jet, he didn't have any instruments or an onboard computer feeding him the data he needed to avoid slamming into the side of a mountain.

"No."

Max closed his eyes. His best shot at killing quickly and without risking any more physical damage to himself required a frontal assault. If he threw small chunks of broken decking into the storage room, maybe even threw it hard enough to hit the door, they would open the door. After all, these invaders had an issue with their curiosity outstripping their tactical good sense.

If Max waited three or four minutes to give the guards time to get into the storage area, he could then open his door and attack. It wasn't a surefire plan, but it was better than his plan for taking out the previous two aliens had been.

James's stubborn streak showed up. "I go with."

"I fight better alone." Guilt gnawed on Max when James's tentacles turned into little curly fries that reminded Max of how upset Rick had been when they thought they might lose Xander.

"I want you safe. I protect you. I can't put you in danger."

"I am cognitively mature."

"I wouldn't care if you were at the end of your lifespan. I would still want to protect you."

James hesitated before asking, "Query. Reason."

Max could've offered any number of explanations. He was trained to defend civilians. He had a bias toward protecting the young. It was a rather unreasonable bias in this part of the universe, but he wasn't ready to let go of his human tendency to shield younger members of sentient races.

But in the end, there was only one reason that mattered. He tangled his fingers with James's tentacles. Xander had always loved the gesture, but James and Kohei were so full of energy that they rarely sat still long enough to embrace Max's hand. But this time James reached out with as many tentacles as he could fit around Max's fingers.

"I gave birth to you. You grew in my body. That makes me your father. It makes me responsible for seeing that you are safe and happy. I will kill every bastard on this ship before I will let them touch you. But I can't do something that puts you in danger. I need you safe."

James tightened his tentacles around Max's hand. "Max goes into more danger."

James wasn't stupid, and Max wasn't going to lie to him. "Yes. I'm going to try to get these two guards to enter the storage area, then I'm going to open this door and fire on them." Max touched the screen to show where he planned on carrying out his attack.

The access passage he would need to use was a vertical shaft with no intersections anywhere close to that deck. If Max had to flee, if the aliens got to that door fast enough, Max would have nowhere to hide. That access shaft was so long that Max had never found the bottom before abandoning his explorations.

"Danger," James said with a little burping noise added at the end.

Maybe it was some sad and lonely piece of his psychology needing to feel loved, but Max imagined that James was distraught. "Yes. That's why you need to stay here."

James pulled his tentacles away from the screen. He tightened his hold on Max's hand before he spoke. "Conditional. If Max is hurt, invaders come for me and brothers and other father."

Bands of fear tightened around Max's chest so much so that he couldn't speak, but he did nod.

James touched the corridor door next to the one where the invaders were guarding. "I need me here. I wait for Max. Conditional. Max fails. I protect. I am cognitively mature."

Max closed his eyes and swallowed. He didn't want to think of James having to pull the trigger. James was his hyperactive little boy, his explorer. He wanted James to grow up and chase skirts and, like his namesake, find peaceful solutions.

However, Max couldn't deny the real danger that he might fail. If that happened, he couldn't leave the rest with no defense at all. Max had seen how fast the children absorbed new ideas, and unfortunately, James had seen him fight. Of everyone on the ship, James was probably best positioned to defend the family.

Max hated it.

Max curled his arm around James's body and leaned in, so that he could rest his forehead against a section of James's oversized head. He was surprised when James allowed the touch. Of the three children, he had always been the least tactile and affectionate. After a second, James pushed him away.

Max tugged on James's leg tentacle, urging him to uncurl it. "You have to protect yourself. Don't let them hurt you," Max said. He pulled on the hand he had intertwined with James's tentacles and drew the second weapon. When he handed it to James, James curled several tentacles around it. "Don't fire if you're too close to them."

"I watch. I learn."

Max nodded and then put James down on the floor. They were close enough to the storage room that James would be able to get himself there. But Max was going to have to do some climbing to reach the access point to the shaft he needed. "Be careful," he told his little explorer.

James made a soft whale sound and then said, "Don't be dead."

That was the best advice Max had ever received.

Chapter Eighteen

F ive dead with one alien left was the thought running through Max's head as he stood outside the door to Rick's control center office. Now that he'd killed the two aliens on the lower level, the computer console showed one bad guy left, and he was standing right next to Rick.

Max hissed and pressed his hand to his right side. He was fairly sure he had pulled a muscle climbing the ladder back out of the service shaft after he'd killed the last two aliens. Much more of this and he was going to be ready for a hospital bed. Hell, he needed one now, but he couldn't afford to reveal the extent of his injuries. James was around the corner, ready to take the fight to the alien leader. That would happen over Max's dead body.

Max raised his weapon before nodding. Around the corner, James opened the door controls he had hacked. Max rushed the room, identifying the enemy. He was too close to Rick, so Max fired. If the asshole took refuge behind Rick, the situation could spin out of control too damn fast.

The invader had been moving toward Rick, but the energy blast shot between him and Rick, and the alien leader leaped backward.

"Max!" Rick shouted. Hopefully none of the blast had hit him, but Max didn't have time to worry about Rick. He kept his weapon focused on the enemy leader while staying far enough back to keep clear of those powerful leg tentacles. Max's stomach still ached from the kick he'd taken from the first asshole he'd killed. The invader stood against the computer console with his short tentacles all pulled up under his body.

"Take your weapon and put it on the floor," Max said. "Carefully. If I even suspect you are trying to use it, I will splatter your guts across the wall."

The invader tilted his pyramid body and looked at Max with those huge eyes. "Query. Confused."

Max took a deep breath. He was running out of energy, but he needed to secure the scene and get information about any potential reinforcements before he crashed. His arms throbbed and his head hurt and black dots swarmed in his vision. "Gun. Floor. Now."

That must have translated because the invader took his weapon out and bent all four of his leg tentacles so he could place his weapon on the floor.

Max tapped the floor with his foot. "Gun. Here. Now."

The invader pushed the weapon with his small tentacles and then stood. "No harm," the invader said. Max wasn't sure if that was a request for mercy or some claim that he hadn't harmed the family. Considering that his men had tried to take an action that would have killed Xander and Kohei, Max didn't feel charitable either way.

"Rick, are you all right?" Max asked, but he kept his gaze on the enemy.

"Yes. I am healthy. There's danger. Other aliens are out there."

"How many?" Max asked. A chorus of whale song blasted the air as James hurried into the room.

James sang at his father for a couple of minutes, and Rick hurried to the computer panel. His tentacles flew across the controls faster than Max could watch, even if he tried. However, Max had more pressing concerns, like not passing out when he was holding a prisoner at gunpoint.

"Max, other aliens are not on sensors. Possibility. They left," Rick said.

James sang to his father again, and this time the computer translated enough words for Max to understand that James was giving him a detailed description of events from the time Max had come to get James in the pool room. Max still hated that he had seen aliens two and three die, but at least he had been around the corner when Max had splattered the guts of aliens four and five all over the storage hold and corridor. At some point they were going to have to get down there and clean up a sizable mess blocking the main doors.

Max asked, "Are there more invaders coming?"

Instead of answering, Rick asked, "Query. Method killing first. He weapon. Max no weapon." Rick's words were choppier than they had been in months.

Once Rick got a question in his head, he tended to focus on it to the point of obsession, so Max answered, "Maintenance hook into internal organs."

The alien commander's eyes grew larger. Good. Maybe the asshole would reconsider his life choices before attacking anyone else's ships and threatening their offspring.

"Rick, I need to know if more of his people are going to rush in here. Where is their ship? James couldn't access external sensors."

"Query. You killed five enemy with one maintenance hook?" Rick was stuck on that part of the story.

"I killed two enemies with two maintenance hooks. I shot the other three." Max raised the weapon since he knew "shot" was not going to translate. Still, something got through because Rick's tentacles quivered and curled up. "Rick," Max said with a sigh, "Focus on the problem. Do we have more enemy coming?"

Rick turned back to the computer and ran his tentacles over the controls. "Enemy ship. Two life forms."

Two. Max figured that would be a pilot and a copilot or perhaps a navigator. But with only two people left on the ship, the enemies Max had killed represented the entire boarding party. Max narrowed his eyes at the pyramid-shaped leader. "So that leaves you. I don't like to kill, but I don't feel safe letting you walk away if you're going to come back for revenge. Rick, any thoughts?"

There was no answer.

Max sighed. Either the translator had large gaps when it came to modern warfare or Rick was still stuck on the idea of Max killing. Or both. Both was pretty damn likely. "Rick, query. What should we do with this enemy? Is he safe to release?"

Rick shuffled closer. "Clarify. Safe for whom? Release is most safe for..." The translator lost the last wailing noise, but Max got the idea.

"Conditional," Max said. "I allow enemy to leave. He returns and harms you, me or the offspring. Query. Conditional true or false?"

"False," the enemy alien said, and his small tentacles twitched. None of these aliens had a poker face, or rather poker tentacles.

"Rick, query, is he telling the truth?" Max needed more information about the enemy, but so far, Rick wasn't cooperating.

"I am unsure." Rick sounded miserable about that admission.

Max took a step back and raised the weapon.

"I no threat. I leave. My ship leave. We leave. No threat," the enemy rushed to say.

Max hesitated. With three people left on the ship, their chances of staging another incursion were low, but Max didn't know whether their ship could take Rick's down.

"Rick, is their ship dangerous?"

"I. Translation matrix failure."

Max gritted his teeth. "James, is the enemy ship dangerous?"

James was so small that he couldn't reach the controls, but he headed for the computer panel. That knocked a little common sense into his father. Rick touched the screen. "Query. Define parameters of dangerous."

"Clarification. Able to damage our ship. Query. Conditional. Enemy ship leaves, it uses weapons on our ship."

"No!" the invader said, his voice high and even more chittery than normal. "No fire. We leave. No danger."

Rick finally found his voice and the ability to speak in coherent sentences. "The enemy ship is too small for significant battle-fighting. Enemy ship is small for attacks without being seen."

"They're raiders who ambush ships," Max said. That suggested they would flee if permitted. At least if they were humans, that's what they would do, but cold fear filled Max's chest because he could be misreading this situation. If he let the leader leave, he might go and find a whole battalion of space ships to attack them.

"Query," Max asked, "will enemy return? Will enemy bring back larger ships?"

"No!" the invader shouted, his tone so high that it hit that nails-on-a-chalkboard note that sent shivers up Max's spine. Either that or shock was setting in and his body temperature was dropping. That was possible. With second degree burn blisters all over his arms and bruises on his bruises, his body wanted to shut down in the worst possible way. Stubbornness was the only force keeping him on his feet.

Max raised his weapon a fraction of an inch. "I can't let you threaten the children."

The invader's smaller tentacles slowly relaxed. Max wondered if it was an intentional gesture, like a human showing his empty hands to appear less threatening. "Query. Children?"

"Offspring," Max clarified. "Humans will not allow their offspring to come to harm. Humans will kill for offspring."

The invader made a show out of looking at James before he again studied Max. "Offspring not human."

Max felt his cold pragmatism give way to hot fury. "I am their father! I am their surrogate father. They grew in me. I've taught them. I've cared for them. They are mine. And I will kill for them." A half-hysterical laugh slipped free, and now Max knew he was going into shock. "Fuck, I would have let you steal whatever information you wanted and stayed with the children, but when you threatened to kill them, I took a hook and disemboweled your people. I would die for the offspring, and I would certainly kill for them."

The invader's tentacles curled back up, and he half turned away so Max could only see one eye.

"If you don't get off this ship right now, I will cut three of your legs off and force you to drag your body through this ship with your one remaining limb. Do not touch a human's offspring!" Max stepped to one side to clear the way for the invader to leave. The alien twitched without leaving. "Go!" Max screamed.

For an awkward, pyramid-shaped alien with a leg under what passed for his face, it could move. He dashed for the door.

When Max's hand trembled, he lowered the weapon and took his finger off the trigger. "Rick, tell me right now if he's dangerous and I need to go kill him."

"No," Rick said. A few of his tentacles uncurled. "No. Can secure door from here. Can watch from here."

"Query. Watch? Show me." Max would feel a lot better if he could see that asshole get off the ship. When he walked over to the display, James "sat" on the floor and reached up with his leg tentacle. Max pulled him up and let him latch onto his neck.

The computer displayed raw data in alien script. "He is leaving," Rick said.

"Clarify. You can monitor from here. To watch requires a picture of what is happening, like the teaching computer downstairs does." Max said.

"Understood. Monitor," Rick repeated. "I can monitor from here. He is leaving. Quickly."

Max snorted. He didn't doubt the asshole was booking it. "I think I need to sit down," Max said. He wanted to get to the couch, but his legs were so unstable that he ended up dropping to the floor. He landed with a thud hard enough to make his teeth clack.

"Max!" James said.

Rick curled his walking tentacle so he was at eye level with Max. "Query. Define the wrong."

Max laughed, and even he could tell there was a touch of hysteria in it. Okay, more than a touch. He pulled at James's tentacle. "Get James to the water."

"No," James said immediately. "Max damaged."

Rick touched Max's arm. Max hissed in pain as a blister burst, sending clear fluid running over his skin. As he'd expected, the burns had gotten a lot worse, and in the crease of his elbows, the skin had broken. Small trails of dried blood ran up his arms. That had happened when he'd been climbing a ladder to get out of an access shaft.

Max should have crossed the storage area and used the door, but the mass of body parts and fluids left behind by aliens four and five had made him avoid the area. He didn't know if he could get sick from contact with alien viscera, but wading through it had seemed unsanitary if not downright dangerous, with his skin damaged. He was going to be more susceptible to infection for a while.

"Query. Size and... of damage."

Max mentally filled in the gap left by the translator as "seriousness" or maybe "nature." He closed his eyes before the black dots swimming in his vision made him more nauseated. "Skin is largest organ. The burn..." the burn was fucking serious. The lower half of both arms was blistered and painful, and the swelling had just started. It would get worse. And then there was the pain low in his abdomen where that asshole had kicked him. Max didn't regret killing that one, not even a little.

"I'm damaged. I need to rest. I need to drink water." The thought of putting anything into his stomach made it roil. Now that the adrenaline was fading, Max felt every injury. He carefully set the weapon to one side without ever opening his eyes.

James sang, and out of the entire belchy, low melody, the only words that came through were "fix," "father" and "Max."

Max opened his eyes and gasped as James's largest eye was millimeters from his nose. That little jolt gave him the energy to reach for the wall. "I think I need to go to the medical facility," Max said. He doubted Rick had much that could help, not when all they could do for Xander was hold him and pray. But hopefully the medical room would be sterile. The largest danger now would be infection.

When Max pushed himself to his feet, his right knee failed. He would have faceplanted, but Rick caught him with a dozen tentacles, at least three of which curled around Max's arms. Max cried out in pain, and Rick loosened his hold. However, he didn't let go. He held Max's waist and pulled his back tight up against his head, and then he moved fast.

Max's legs dangled inches above the floor, and he felt a little like a puppy that had peed and whose owner had grabbed it under the elbows before rushing it outside, the whole time holding it out in front. However, compared to something like a fireman's hold, he was almost not in pain. The tentacles around his bruised middle didn't feel great, but at least Rick wasn't touching his arms.

"Wait. James?" Max looked around. James had vanished, and Max didn't want Rick to accidentally step on the little guy. However, Rick rushed him out into the corridor too fast for Max to see where James had gone. "You have to get James to water," Max reminded Rick. The grunting noise he got back wasn't comforting, but Rick loved his offspring. Max assumed he wouldn't do something stupid like forgetting to put them back in the water. "Oh, Xander and Kohei are in the filter room. They need help getting back up to the pool."

Rick continued to ignore him, and Max sighed. He wasn't strong enough to fight his way free of Rick's tentacles, that was for sure. They turned a corner and headed down the corridor that led to the medical room. At least they weren't taking the hallway where Max had left two of the bodies. Max had gotten good at seeing the silver lining.

Chapter Nineteen

Max woke to a terrible itching in both arms. After prying his eyes open, he saw both arms covered in snot or something vaguely snot-like. Either the stuff had serious healing powers or Max had been unconscious for quite a while. His arms were pink and hairless, but the worst of the burn had healed.

He struggled to sit up. "Rick?" Max looked around at the small medical room. Everything was tucked away and the room was as neat as ever. Of course it was. He hadn't shot any aliens here. Certain other parts of the ship were probably a mess, and Max should clean that up before the kids saw it. Maybe Max had destroyed James's youthful innocence, but Kohei and Xander didn't need to see dead bodies.

When Max swung his legs off the side of the exam table, his stomach muscles complained. Loudly. Well that answered one question, because he was still bruised and sore. He raised the hem of his shirt and winced at the vivid reds and purples that covered his skin. They hadn't had time to turn green. One of those Marines had had always made fun of could have done better. His only consolation was that the asshole who had kicked him would be dead a whole lot longer than Max would be bruised.

His hand-to-hand combat instructors would be proud. Shocked, but proud.

"Max!" Rick came around the corner, one side of his oversized hat crumpled. Max felt another wave of rage at that reminder of the violence they had all suffered. "You awaken."

"Clarify. Woke up. 'Awaken' is too formal." Max rubbed a hand over his face.

Rick stopped at the doorway to the medical room. "Query. We are not formal?"

Max snorted. Considering where Rick had put his tentacles, they were on a first-name basis. "I was surrogate for your children. We passed formal a long time ago." Max lowered himself to the floor, and the pain didn't increase. That was a good sign. "Thank you for treating the burns." Max held up his arms.

"Energy damage," Rick said.

"Yes, I was there when I damaged them." Max frowned. "Query. Where are the weapons?" The offspring might be cognitively mature, but so were the men and women in boot camp, and no one had trusted them with live ammunition until they had been drilled on safety until their hair fell out. Even then, training accidents happened. Too damn many. Cognitive maturity did not preclude stupidity.

"I placed in secure storage. Query. Will I bring you a weapon?"

Max leaned back against the table. He didn't want to feel like he needed to walk around the ship armed, but after the invasion, he had to admit he felt a little vulnerable. "Do I need one? Query. Will more invaders come?"

Rick gave a low, rumbling trumpet before saying, "That ship never return."

"Query. How did they get in your ship?" Max asked.

Instead of answering, Rick curled a couple of his longer tentacles so the orange-red tips dangled under his head. "You are warrior."

Something was bothering him. Max set the issue of invasions aside for the moment. "I told you that."

Rick's tentacles twitched. Max waited for Rick to say something. He didn't. Eventually Max said, "Yes, I am a warrior. I'm a fighter pilot. I prefer to fight using machines, but I trained to fight with my hands." At the time, his instructors had been more concerned about pilots having to bail out of aircraft behind enemy lines, since alien invaders hadn't been on the table as a serious discussion. One disabled captain had taught a class on improvised defensive weaponry by creating imaginary scenarios that included aliens and vampires, but everyone who took the class agreed that Captain Evans had been trying to avoid sounding like a racist by having them prepare for jihad terrorists. Now Max wondered.

"I didn't set the statement to truth."

"Ah." That made sense. "Clarify. Correction. You thought I lied." Max leaned back against the exam table.

"Yes. Lied. I thought you lied." Rick stretched out his tentacles and then squiggled them back up again.

Max sighed. "I didn't. I worked hard to become a fighter pilot. I don't like to kill, but I trained to protect my home."

"You are a warrior," Rick repeated.

This was getting a little obsessive, even for Rick. "Query. Why do you care?"

Rick slid into the room and curled a tentacle around the nearest support leg on the exam table. "I hired a warrior to surrogate offspring for compensation." Rick trumpeted and curled two tentacles.

"I accepted compensation to surrogate. I love Kohei and James and Xander."

"Query. Clarify love."

This was territory Max didn't know how to navigate. He wanted the children healthy and successful. He felt pride when they handled a situation with cool efficiency, and Max didn't normally internalize others' performance. He felt all that and more for Rick. The children were... well... children. But Rick was sweet and caring and not a child. And Max had no idea how to explain any of the various forms of love he felt for the family. He said something that Rick would understand. "I would kill for them."

Rick trumpeted again. It was a noise Max hadn't heard often. Rick then added, "You did kill for them."

"Yep. Hopefully the pirates won't come back."

"Unintelligent energy shapes," Rick said with an unhappy belch.

"Energy shape? Clarify." The translator had missed that one.

Rick touched the computer and a screen appeared. The general display switched to the curved and expanded alien version of a periodic table. Rick chose an element on the lower right side and selected it. A structure with dozens of electrons zipping around the central nucleus appeared and then a yellowish brown rock appeared, and then an image of the refined metal. It had crystalized into squares that dully reflected the light. Luckily chemistry had always been Max's favorite class.

"Polonium. They're stupid polonium-headed pirates," Max translated. He would have gone for poopy heads. He would not associate the pirates with something as deadly as polonium, not when an unarmed prisoner could take out their entire boarding party. But insults didn't seem to translate well.

"Stupid polonium-headed pirates," Rick echoed. "Query. You are warrior and you accepted compensation for surrogacy."

Max assumed that Rick wanted to know why. "Can we have this discussion after I pee?" he asked. He hoped that would send Rick running. He avoided bodily fluids as a general rule. However, Rick simply watched. Silently. Slightly creepily.

With a sigh, Max headed for the recycling unit. He pulled out the low drawer-like trough and peed. The pain made him hiss and he had a touch of pink in with the yellow. He had taken a body blow, but if something important had ruptured or cracked, he would have felt worse.

"Query. Have you cleaned up the bodies?" Max asked.

"I discarded without cleaning. Query. Do humans have rituals for cleaning dead before removal?"

Max huffed. "Yeah, we do."

"Regrets. I did not clean first," Rick said. "Apologies."

"Clarify. We clean our dead. We discard the dead of enemies. I was asking if the ship was clean."

"The ship is clean. I removed personal shielding and weapons. I can bring you items salvaged from enemy you killed."

Max nodded. He assumed that was a peace offering, but there was something he wanted more—a subject he was stuck on as firmly as Rick seemed stuck on the idea that Max was a warrior. Once he finished peeing and breathing through the pain, Max folded the piss trough back into the wall and opened the hatch to the sink. "Query. Why were the invaders here?"

"To invade."

Max imagined the "no-duh" tone Rick was probably using in his own language. After he finished washing his hands, Max pushed the sink back into the wall and headed for the door. This shirt had alien blood and viscera or something on it, and it was torn in several places. He'd talked the computer into producing one spare and now he hoped he could convince the computer to fabricate another one because he'd gotten used to having a spare on washing day. "I need to change shirts," Max said as he passed Rick.

Part of him expected Rick to leave and go back to his control room. He wasn't willing to talk to Max about the invaders, and Max wasn't sure what he wanted to know about Max's past as a service member. Instead, Rick followed him down the corridor. However, he kept a far greater distance than Max was used to.

Rick was a pretty touchy-feely alien. Even after the offspring had been born, he'd tended to swim or walk within tentacle reach. More than once, he'd rested one of his light green tentacles on Max's shoulder, allowing the red tip to dangle. Rick had explained that thousands of years ago, his people had used the red color to attract prey, but now it was decorative. He'd explained that he was quite proud of how much red he had on his tentacles. Apparently, Rick was a real looker.

Once in his quarters, Max left the door open as an invitation. Instead of coming all the way into the small room, Rick hovered near the door. The change in Rick's behavior bothered Max more than he would have expected. He hoped that he hadn't ended their easy friendship by showing how willing he was to kill. Max didn't regret what he had done; he'd saved the children. But he did wish he could have found another method.

"Query. You are a warrior and you accepted compensation for surrogate."

Max sighed. Rick was going to stay stuck on that point until they had this discussion. Rick had a quick fantasy of siccing Major Jones on him. When some idiot airman had commented on her being a kickass pilot yet taking time off for her kid's birthday party, she had verbally striped the skin from his hide. That woman had been five-foot-three of muscle and attitude. "I am a warrior. I am surrogate father for your offspring. I am both."

Rick blurbled. That was a new noise and Max tentatively labelled it confusion. The other alternatives were distress or fear, but Max never wanted Rick to feel that around him. However, the sudden distance between them suggested Rick's comfort level had dropped.

Max pulled the edge of the bunk down and sat on it. The bunks were mere inches off the floor, so the position required Max to look up at Rick. "I am far from my people. I don't know the strengths or weaknesses of any race. I do not know weapons or security systems. I cannot hire myself out as a warrior. The two offers for compensation were surrogate or translation. You compensated more."

"Impossible. Fee for translation of warrior species is valuable."

"Yeah, apparently not," Max said with a shrug. And ironically, he had ended up doing the translation work anyway, at least on Rick's computer. "I would have needed to work for centuries to earn enough money to get back to my planet of birth."

Rick whistled. "They offer you compensation for child's language."

"I think the translation matrix failed. I am not a child."

Rick whistled and settled down farther so he was eye to eye with Max, although he stayed well out of tentacle reach. "Our offspring are not children. They lack experience, but they have cognitive ability."

"Query. Clarify. Are you using child to mean lacking in cognitive ability?"

Rick rotated his body to consider Max out of a new set of eyes. "Yes."

That did explain why Rick would get so twitchy when Max called the offspring children. "Clarify. Child means offspring when they are small."

"Clarify. Child means offspring who lack cognitive ability or species who lacks cognitive ability."

Max rubbed a hand over his face. He had screwed up that bit of translation. "Clarify. Child is only for offspring."

"Query. The word for those who lack cognitive ability."

Max thought about that for a moment. He was tempted to shoot off at the mouth and say idiot, but then if Rick's people ever reached Earth, they'd call some baby an idiot, and that would not end well. "If the individual will grow into cognitive ability later, they are immature. If they will never grow into cognitive ability we would say they are..." Max mentally sorted through his many, many choices. "Simple," he settled on. "Unless we don't like them. Then we call them a moron."

"Earth children are immature. Query. Correct or not?"

"Correct," Max said. "Query, were they offering me payment based on my language being simple?"

"They offered compensation for language of morons."

Max blinked. They invaded his fucking world and then assumed his people lacked cognitive abilities? That was illogical and just plain rude.

"They visited my world. They saw jets and cities and civilizations based on cognitive abilities. They had to know that humans are intelligent creatures."

"Their logic is…" Rick's last word was lost in translation, but Max could fill in the blanks. "If you as individual could not solve problems, then you as individual is a moron."

"I want to go back and punch Heetayu." Max leaned back, bracing himself on his elbows as he lounged. Maybe he was being a little obvious—making himself look less dangerous—but he needed Rick to see nothing had changed. He wasn't kidding about Heetayu, though. Those bastards had invaded his world, and when he had been confused and panicked, they assumed that made him a moron. They deserved an ass kicking.

"I would rather overcharge them for gathering of new translation matrix." Rick moved to the side of the bunk and rested several tentacles on the edge of it. "They will pay for translation of language with warriors. Not all species produce warriors."

"Few humans are warriors," Max said. Some days he questioned his own suitability. Back on Earth, he had been ashamed of how grateful he was that the advent of drones meant that he was less likely to pull the trigger on an enemy. He hadn't wanted to take a life. He had, but he hadn't wanted to. And his shame came from his relief that some poor drone pilot sitting at a computer in the Midwest would have to push the button, and that poor schmuck wouldn't even get combat pay for doing it.

"You are one," Rick said. He lowered himself by curling his leg tentacle into a neat coil on the floor. "Warriors do not respect me."

Max blew out a long breath. That was a rather broad and depressing statement, one that broke his heart a little. When those invaders had held Rick at gunpoint, Max had been nearly homicidal. He hadn't understood how much he cared about Rick until that point, and now Rick questioned whether Max respected him at all.

"I respect you," Max said slowly so the translator would get every word. He needed Rick to understand this. "I respect how you exhausted yourself caring for Xander. You are an incredible father. I respect your skills that allow you to afford such a nice ship. However you earn your compensation, you are effective. I respect you for being so honest and having so much patience with me. When I got here, I didn't understand much, and you helped me with the computer and how to use the bathroom and how to open doors. At one point I thought you didn't care about me, that you only cared about the offspring I carried, and it hurt," Max confessed. He remembered sitting in the access shafts crying. Not his finest moment.

"Clarify pain."

Max closed his eyes. "I hurt because I do like you. I respect you. I thought you liked me, but then when I found out about the surrogacy, I thought I was wrong. I thought you didn't like me. It turns out, you thought I was a liar." Max laughed. His feelings were one big tangled mess. He didn't know what he felt. He did know Rick's touchy-feely period hadn't ended when Max had given birth. Rick had been just as quick to touch or to share conversation after the offspring were born. And now Rick wouldn't come close.

Max wondered if this was what the soldiers from Vietnam had felt like when they'd come home and had been called baby killers. Rick acted as if Max was suddenly someone different—someone dangerous and unstable.

"I was wrong. You are not lying. You are a warrior," Rick said. He reached out as if he wanted to touch Max, but then he pulled his tentacle back.

Max grimaced. He hated this new distance between them, but he would never regret protecting the family. Now that he had nearly lost them, Max could admit to himself that he felt like these people were his family just as much as Pete and his parents were.

Rick rotated his whole body to watch Max out of a different set of eyes.

Maybe it was time to change the subject. Max leaned forward. "Query. What did invaders hope to take?"

"Query. Reason for knowing." Rick had his paranoia dialed up to ten, and his reluctance didn't make Max feel any more warm or fuzzy.

"Answer. I want to know what to defend. I want to know who else might come."

Rick inched closer, but the silence was pretty telling. He didn't want to tell Max what the bad guys wanted.

"Query," Max asked, "do you have something illegal on this ship? Something dangerous?"

"No," Rick said immediately. "No additional ships will come. I move ship farther from developed planets. Too expensive to pursuit. You do not need to be a warrior."

Max was starting to form a few hypotheses. "I am always a warrior. I can't stop being one, even when I have offspring in me. I will always protect you and the offspring."

Rick's tentacles twitched. "You protected offspring. Humans have imperative with surrogate offspring." He had left himself out of that list of people Max would protect. And actually, he had reduced all of Max's efforts to a biological imperative. Max had issues with that.

He leaned forward and rested his elbows on his knees, appreciating again how good the burn cream was. He didn't have a single blister—just some pink, healing skin. "Some humans fight to protect others. Some humans hurt others. Most humans protect offspring. Some don't." Max thought about the assistant football coach who had been arrested for child porn. He'd had a long conversation with his brother, and he remembered the fear that the man might have touched Petey. "Humans rarely prey on offspring," Max added after a pause. Rick's tentacles all curled up, which was fair because that's how Max felt about pedophiles. "Query. Are all your people the same?"

"No," Rick said slowly. "But no my people are warriors. We hunt from secrecy."

"Some of my people do that too," Max said. "This is not about humans. This is about me. I would always protect you. I would always protect the offspring." As Max said the words, he felt a tightening in his chest at the idea of someone threatening his adopted family. In the past, Rick had always been the one to initiate touch, so Max took a risk. He held one of Rick's tentacles. "The invaders deserved to die because they would have hurt the family. I only killed them because of that."

Rick curled his tentacle around Max's wrist. "Clarify. Family is a genetically related grouping of individuals."

"Correction." Max squeezed Rick's tentacle. "Family is grouping of individuals committed to helping each other without seeking compensation." Maybe that wasn't the most linguistically accurate definition, but it described how Max felt about the people on this ship.

Rick tightened his hold on Max's wrist. "Invaders want me. I create numbers that computers use."

"Clarify. You're a programmer," Max said.

"Programmer," Rick echoed. "I computer programmer for instructions that..." At this point the translator completely broke down, but Max could think of a number of different endings for that sentence. Rick could be involved in cybersecurity or weapons development or any number of other valuable fields. Hell, maybe Max was sitting in a room with the alien version of Tony Stark. Max considered Rick and the shy way he held Max's wrist and inched closer bit by bit.

Maybe not. Rick was far too shy to be Iron Man.

Rick continued. "I thought ship safe. I thought I hidden my work."

Max didn't need to understand the various belches to hear the guilt. "I should have killed the last guy," Max said.

Rick blasted a whale song. "Better this way," Rick said. "He will tell others that humans are terror-causing and violent to defend offspring. Scare universe. They treat you like moron, so they deserve terror."

Max laughed. "You have a mean streak."

Rick twirled slowly. "No streak. Just mean."

Max's laughter grew so wild that he collapsed back onto his bunk. That was the sort of meanness Max could get behind.

Chapter Twenty

Max walked into the pool room, trying to ignore the sudden distance between himself and Rick. Rick followed several steps behind, and until this moment, Max had not realized how he had grown used to having Rick hovering at his elbow all the time, even after the offspring were born. Sure, there was a period where they spent almost no time together because they were taking shifts with Xander. At most one of them had sat at the edge of the pool and talked.

But when Xander had gotten large enough to push them away and swim on his own, they had fallen back into their old patterns. When Max had given up on translations for the day, he would get into the pool with the kids, and Rick would show up shortly after.

The minute Max saw Kohei spinning in circles, the tightness in his chest eased. He stripped off his shirt as he walked toward the pool. "Hey kids, looking good," he called out.

Three translator voices using three different pitches all cried out, "Max!"

Max slipped out of his pants so that he could get in the water, but James was already out and reaching for him. "Max Father, I told them. I told them how you..." At that point, the computer failed and all Max heard was whale song. He needed to spend some time with the translation matrix trying to define the more violent end of the universe. Maybe the work would distract him from the guilt of exposing James to that sort of brutality.

James curled his tentacles around Max's wrist. Xander slapped the pool with his long tentacles and Kohei abandoned his pirouettes. When Max waded in, the offspring crowded near. Max turned around to look at Rick, who still kept a certain distance, although he was inching closer.

"Rick Father," Xander called. He ran his tentacles across Max's arm before he swam for his father.

Rick quickly entered the water and pulled Xander close.

"Your father's work is valuable. Now I know I have to keep him safe," Max said. He could only hope that time would help Rick get more comfortable with the idea that Max was a warrior. Everything Max had done was to protect the family, so it felt unfair that his actions had put an emotional distance between them.

James let go of Max and swam over to his father, where he curled his tentacles around Rick's. "I help. I protect Rick Father and Xander Sibling and Kohei Sibling."

"You were much help." Rick curled his tentacles around his son. Kohei had glommed onto Max's left hand, but now he launched himself toward his father. Max smiled as he watched them all crowd around Rick. The offspring were not the most social children in all creation, so it felt nice to see them connecting. After a second, Xander's tentacles escaped the general mass and started reaching for Max.

Half-afraid that Rick would retreat from him, Max moved closer. Xander stretched until he could wrap his tentacles around Max's arm. Then Xander pulled with significantly more strength than Max had realized the little one possessed. The next thing Max knew, he was engulfed by tentacles as Xander drew him closer. It felt good.

And cold.

"Query. Did someone reduce the temperature on the pool?" Max asked.

Rick answered. "Invaders wanted conservation of energy to recharge their ship."

The offspring shifted and Max was pulled closer until pressed up against Rick's warm central head. "You do have the heat turned up, though, right? Query?"

"I do," Rick agreed. He raised a tentacle as if expecting Max to flee. Eventually he wrapped it around Max's waist.

The offspring had claimed Max's left hand and his entire arm was wrapped in tentacles, but he reached around with his right to embrace Rick. When he touched something slick, the folds of skin warned him that he had touched Rick's eyeball. Rick was smooth everywhere except where his tentacles met his body and around his eyes. "I'm sorry," Max blurted.

"Query. What do you regret?" Rick tried withdrawing his tentacle, but Kohei wrapped his own tentacles around it, holding Rick in place.

"I regret touching your eye," Max said. "I apologize for touching your eye."

The eye closest to Max dilated. "Eyes are to be touched."

"Seriously?" A full-body shudder ran through Max.

No one answered him, but given that Max had not properly marked the question he wasn't surprised. He tried again. "Clarify. Human eyes are not for touching. Query. Can I touch the eyes of the people?"

"Understood. I will not touch your eyes," Rick said. "You may touch my eyes with comfort." Rick tightened his tentacle around Max's waist again.

And there they were, right back to the alien and bizarre conversations they'd had before invaders had decided to attack the ship. Max leaned into Rick's head and shivered. Rick might be a wonderful hot water bottle, but Max's limbs were still slowly losing feeling.

"Are the offspring safe in such cold water?"

"I am cold, cold. Kohei warm. Kohei keep me warm," Xander said with a hnng-hnng noise added onto the end.

"I warm too." James crawled over Max's shoulder, lifting himself out of the water to perch on Max's head.

"James is warm on land," Xander complained.

"I am warm enough for Xander," Kohei said, and that ended the escalations. Max smiled. It had sounded so much like him and Petey fighting over the Halloween candy that it was hard to believe he was on an alien ship.

"I think I am too cold to stay in the water," Max said. He shivered. While he should swim to the edge, he hated leaving the little island of warmth he had found. But if he didn't, his toes might freeze off. He had enough problems with potential kidney bruising, so he didn't need to add frostbite. Max started to pull away from the family puppy pile.

James stayed on his head for a few seconds before he slid off, but when Max kicked his legs to swim toward the edge of the pool, Rick hung on. Max had to swim with his feet because Rick held so tightly all the way to firm ground, where Rick released him. "Query. Option. You may choose new living section," Rick said.

Max stopped at the edge of the water and turned to look at him. That had come out of nowhere. "Query. Why would I want a new room?" Max asked. It had taken him time to learn to use all the latches and knobs in the room he had. Even though Rick had been quick to offer his help with any of the equipment, Max's pride had prevented him from taking up too much of Rick's time. Trial and error had allowed him to figure out most of the features, although Rick had to help Max with the use of bathroom.

"Come." Rick headed for the door at warp speed.

Max blew out a breath. Rick was excited about something.

"Rick Father warmed Max Father," Xander said.

Max grabbed the thin fabric Rick had manufactured after Max had described a towel.

"I was not dangerously cold," Max said, "Not unless I stayed in the water much longer. Query. Do you need more warmth?" Max was uncomfortable leaving Xander in such cold water.

"Kohei is warm," Xander said. "Air is warm."

Max assumed that meant Xander could warm up by getting out of the water. "James, help with warmth," Max said.

James hit the surface of the water with a tentacle. "Xander be warm!" he said loudly as Max was putting his pants on. Max didn't know whether the clever little git was avoiding making a promise to help keep his brother warm or if that was a poorly worded vow. Max would come back and check on them soon, but he had to trust that Xander could speak up if he needed more help.

Grabbing his shirt off the chair as he passed, Max followed Rick through the pool room door closest to the control room.

The corridor was empty, but Max turned right. His instincts were still sharp because he found Rick halfway to the control room.

"Hurry, hurry," Rick said before he headed for the lift. Max broke into a trot. Rick's excitement was infectious. Max smiled as he crowded onto the lift with Rick's oversized head. They went up one level and then the lift opened onto the corridor right outside the control room.

Rick placed a tentacle at Max's back and urged him forward. Max frowned, but he followed Rick's tacit suggestion and touched the control to open the door. Back when he'd been exploring the ship, he'd found this door locked every time. Now it opened. Max raised an eyebrow and headed into the control room.

"Go, go go," Rick said. He was spinning slowly, which reminded Max of Kohei and his pirouettes. Max followed the gentle pushes to a door on the other side. Now they were in a section that Max had seen on the computer diagram that James had displayed. None of the access shafts led to this part of the ship, or at least none of the ones large enough for a human did. And as far as Max could tell, the only access was through the command room.

The second they entered the new area, Max could immediately tell the difference.

The corridors were wider, the floor softer. Instead of the simple grayish white color that dominated the lower ship, this deck had colors—blues and greens and grays that swirled together in a way that made Max think of water. Even the lights overhead flickered and wavered in a way that reminded him of sunlight as it filtered through the lake when he was a child and swam under its surface. Max ran his hand across the wall.

"Query. Color preference?" Rick asked.

"I prefer this. It's beautiful," Max said.

Rick shimmied. "I chose designs. I fabricated colors and lights."

"You created a feeling like water without water. It is impressive." Max meant it. This part of the ship had a soul in a way that the rest didn't. The lower decks were functional, not beautiful. Rick gave a quarter turn and then continued down the hallway, but he kept his largest eye on Max.

Max ran his hand along the wall. There were slight texture differences between the metallic gray and the shimmery blue and the soft green. Rick had chosen different materials rather than applying a color on a single material. It was stunning.

They entered the lift, and a large red jellyfish creature decorated the upper corner. Max touched one of the long tendrils that hung down from the bell-shaped body. They were far thinner than Rick's or even the children's tentacles, and the body appeared far too insubstantial to hold anything approaching a brain. "Query. Is this from your home world?"

"Yes."

"It looks like a jellyfish from my world."

Rick touched the figure with a single tentacle before saying, "They are most dangerous."

"So are jellyfish," Max said. It was strange to think that two planets light years apart with dominant species as different as him and Rick could have such similar animal life.

Then again, maybe all inhabited planets had some version of a jellyfish. Certainly tentacles were more common than boned limbs, so it made sense that jellyfish would be more common than horses. Max wondered what these people would think of a horse... or giraffe. Having a little tiny head so far away from the body would have to seem strange to beings that had, for the most part, developed a head and body structure that was joined. Max figured they thought he looked pretty funny with a weird sticklike neck separating the two.

Rick stopped near a metallic teal ripple and touched the pad to open the door. "Option. You sleep here."

Rick moved to one side and Max walked into the room. It was substantially larger and sections of wall stuck out, almost like someone had hung cabinets and forgot to add doors.

Max walked to the far wall where the bed had been in his own quarters. It had the same sorts of abstract swirls, only greens and yellows interrupted the shades of blue. It reminded Max a little of pictures of Earth from space. "It's beautiful."

"Explore," Rick said.

Maybe Max was developing a vivid imagination, but he could've sworn Rick sounded proud. He should've been. He had an incredible ship. Max felt for seam that would lower the Murphy bed structure. It took him a second because the seam was up higher than he'd expected, right underneath the cabinets. Max triggered the latch and then stepped back as the sleeping platform took over the space. The room was larger, but the bed was close to a queen-size, so with the bed down there was still a lack of open space.

"Emergency supplies," Rick said, and he pointed toward the area underneath the cabinets. Max sat on the bed and the surface yielded like the most expensive mattress in creation. He'd had a hookup on a thousand-dollar mattress once, and this thing made that seem like a Wal-mart hide-a-bed.

When Max looked up into the underside of the "cabinets," mechanical controls and gauges covered the surface. Max reached up, hoping that if he was about to hit an emergency fire suppression system or something that Rick would stop him. His fingers hit glass or a cool plastic of some sort before he could touch any of the controls.

"In emergency cover withdraws," Rick said. He climbed onto the bed next to Max. Max spotted a number of deep storage cubbyholes, but he didn't own anything besides one spare pair of pants, but he could have fit his entire wardrobe from back home into it. He had the feeling that these quarters were intended for either officers or family members.

"This is a nice room," Max said. Something in his soul warmed at the idea that Rick wanted him to live in the private half of the ship. "Thank you."

Rick gave another all-tentacle shimmy that meant he was happy, Max would never say it to Rick's face, but it reminded Max of the way his family dog would get excited when people came home. Snoopy had often given that same full body shimmy at the door. Max ran his hand along Rick's tentacle. It quickly curled around Max's wrist.

"You can stay here weeks three," Rick said.

His brain on automatic, Max was about to correct the word order, but the meaning of the words registered, and he swallowed. The easy joy of a few seconds ago suddenly developed a darker edge. It was like someone had turned on the dum-da-da background music and clouds had covered the sun. Metaphorically, anyway.

"Query. Why would I only stay here three weeks?" Max tried to pull his hand away, but Rick had a good hold on his wrist.

"Max desires return to Earth."

Max had to clear his throat before he could get words out. "Query. What are you saying?"

Rick leaned closer. "Clarify. Max desires to return to Earth."

"Rick, I know what I want. I'm asking why you say I'm only going to be here three weeks." Max's heart pounded at the idea being dropped at some alien port of call. Of course he should find another job and start earning money. He had an obligation to return to Earth and to the Air Force. There were even rules about it. And sure, the surrogate job was over, but he hadn't expected Rick to leave him. He wasn't sure how he had gone from being part of the family and getting invited into the inner sanctum to getting his ass dropped off at some space station because the job was over.

Rick uncurled his tentacle from around Max's wrist. "Ship reaches the Earth planet in three weeks."

The bottom fell out of Max's world. "What? This ship? Query. Will this ship be at Earth in three weeks?"

"Yes."

Max froze. His brain just stopped working. For months now, all he had thought about was learning to function in the universe to earn enough credits to be able to get back home. He'd damn near cried from homesickness, and he had never been one of those guys that talked about home the way Forrest Gump's buddy talked about shrimp. Nope. Not him. But now that he was faced with the prospect of going home in three weeks, he didn't know how he felt. He knew he didn't feel particularly good. Home. His brain couldn't process the word.

"I take Max to Earth," Rick said, and the bastard sounded proud of himself.

Chapter Twenty-One

Max shifted away, but Rick's tentacles followed, pulling at him. "Query. Physiological changes in your bodily function?" Rick asked.

"That's a good question. As soon as I figure out what I'm feeling. I'll let you know." Max laughed weakly.

"Query. Do you seek to see more better?" Rick asked.

"What?" Max blinked at Rick, not sure he was following the conversation, but then this whole day was turning out to be one long exercise in confusion and frustration.

"Clarify. The window of your eye has increased. You breathe more rapidly and eye movements have increased. Query. Do you seek to see more better?"

Ignoring Rick's question, Max asked, "Why are we going to Earth?"

Despite the fact that Rick normally stuck to his questions with the tenacity of a two-year-old, Rick answered. "I believed I camouflaged my identity. I failed. I must take ship away until offspring are older. I cannot risk them. Earth is isolated. Quiet."

That was disturbingly logical. Fatherly. Uncondemnable, and yet Max wanted to find some reason to attack Rick for making such a precipitous decision. "Earth had a high-speed intergalactic chase through their backyard," he pointed out.

"Isolated incident. No one visits that part of space. No trade. Quiet," Rick said, "for offspring."

For offspring. Max couldn't argue against any action that would protect them. Max stared at the far wall. It was so damn logical, and Rick did like his logic. Three weeks. He had three more weeks to father the children and play with the translation computer. And then he would go back to being Captain Max Davis, Air Force.

Or not.

The world would be different, and Max would be the man who came back from alien space. With an alien. He'd be a bigger freak than when he'd been the only openly gay kid in his high school. He'd be on the outside again, like when he'd first joined the Air Force at the tail end of Don't Ask, Don't Tell. Even after the President had lifted the policy, Max had lived in fear that someone would reverse the reversal or that some superior officer would punish him for being gay.

Now he would be the freak who had lived with aliens. Who had given birth to aliens. He suspected the whole process had caused one or two physical changes. And the sort of exam the human doctors would subject him to would spot them.

So he had all sorts of reasons to avoid Earth, but those weren't the worst. His chest hurt at the idea of leaving the children behind, at leaving Rick behind. He'd grown used to getting in water fights, fights he lost spectacularly because beings with umpteen tentacles had far more splash power than a human. Yet the second Max surrendered, Rick would stop. He would reach out and touch him as if to make sure that Max was okay. And that closeness had continued after the children were born.

If anything, Rick had been more solicitous after the children came. He trusted Max to hold Xander, to keep him warm. Hell, he used the names Max had chosen. When the kids called one another "Xander" and "James" and "Kohei," Max expected indignation or hurt feelings if not outright anger. Instead, Rick had asked what the names meant. Each of the kids had been quick to tell their father the stories Max had shared with them.

And Rick had been interested. It drove home the point that Max had dated too damn many men who cared about sex but didn't give a shit about talking. Max liked having a shipmate he could talk to.

Rick tightened his hold on Max's arm. "Query. Physiological responses?"

Max's laugh was low and rough. "I'm not sure." The joy he'd expected at the idea of going home was MIA.

"Query. How can you ignorance your physiological responses?"

"Query. You're calling me a moron for not knowing how I'm feeling, aren't you?"

"Max not moron," Rick said sharply, using questionable grammar. He then wrapped two additional tentacles around Max's arm.

That made Max smile despite his foul mood. "Sometimes I am." Max sighed. He missed his parents and Pete the way he would miss a limb. He missed pizza and soda and football and figure skating. He'd had tickets to Hamilton, and he'd hated missing that.

And music. He missed the hell out of music. He even missed being an Air Force pilot. Sure, he'd bitched about the hours and the paperwork and the annoying people he worked with, but he loved flying, and he was proud of the work he did for his country. He wanted all those back, but he didn't want Earth.

"I don't know if I want to go home to Earth," Max confessed. He hated the idea that the planet probably thought they had been invaded by an enemy armada. His parents would have mourned him and now lived in fear that the invaders could return any time. He didn't want humans to live in fear. People deserved to know that they were in the boring end of the universe and no one would bother with them. But did he want to be the person who lived on Earth all the time? That wasn't even a close call. "I am a horrible person for not wanting to go home."

"Query. Clarify horrible. Query. Do humans required a return to birth place?" Rick pressed close.

"You mean, are we like salmon?" Max asked. He had an image of a fish with a man's head. Or maybe that should be a man with a fish head. "Clarify. Humans are not required to return. However, good humans care about their home and do want to go home. I do not want to go home. Conclusion. I am horrible."

Rick was silent for a time, and Max stewed in his own guilt. He had lied to Rick because he was required to go home. The Code of Conduct required him to escape as soon as possible and return to the nearest American military facility. When he'd taken this job, that's what he had been trying to do. Only now he found that three weeks was far too soon for him to return.

"The people do not return to the place of birthing. We move with waves. On and forward and on," Rick said. "When Kohei and James and Xander grow large enough, they will leave and not return."

"I hate that idea," Max said.

"I am in agreement," Rick said. "I am happy the offspring will require several years of tending before offspring have skills to earn compensation other places."

Anger caught Max like a knife under his ribs. Rick got years; Max got three weeks.

Rick shifted closer until his tentacles spilled over Max's thigh and his stupid, floppy hat hit the side of Max's head. "Query. Is human fathering an imperative, motivating you to stay with offspring?"

"That's part of it," Max admitted. "I know they're cognitively mature, but they're so small, and they don't understand how shitty people can be." Although they had gotten an unfortunate crash course during the invasion.

"Clarify. Query. Do not all creatures produce excrement?"

Max's brain was locked in first gear, because it took him a second to connect excrement to shittiness. Rick's literalness would have made him a great foil on some sitcom. "Clarify. Shitty means horrible and undesirable. It implies a person's actions are as disagreeable as fresh excrement in plain sight."

"That is wonderfully descriptive." Rick's tentacles shimmied. "Shitty. I approve."

Despite his foul mood, Rick's delight made Max smile. "I'm glad you like my profanity."

"I like much of you Max, although Earth fathers are weird."

"It is not weird to protect offspring."

"No." Rick leaned against Max. "I came to this space because I too wish to protect offspring. But protecting offspring is genetic for the people. Human fathers attach genetic imperatives to emotional connections." Rick hesitated before adding, "I like weird."

"Then you'd love Earth," Max said dryly.

"Earth quiet. I can camouflage offspring on Earth. Max can protect offspring."

Horror stole all Max's words for a moment before he shouted. "What? No!"

Rick jerked all his tentacles away.

"You can't come to Earth. People are so quick to judge." Max burst up and made it to the door before he whirled back around. "You have to promise you will never take the boys to Earth. People hate each other for having the wrong skin color or being born on the wrong continent or for believing something different about supernatural beings that can't be proven to exist at all. If you come in with your tentacles and your... tentacles. No. You have to stay away." Max ran out of air, but the panic still raged through his guts.

Rick slid off the bed and approached slowly. "Query. Clarify. Humans' feelings toward the people."

Fuck. Max hadn't wanted to get into any of his planet's irrational responses. However, if he had to out the assholish nature of humans to protect Rick and the boys, he would. "Humans fear. A lot. Before the ships came to Earth, my people believed they were alone. Maybe they hoped they were alone. But now... I don't know how they have reacted since I left, but I know you will never be safe there."

"I am not warrior. Human planet one of warriors. I will keep away," Rick said. The translator voice didn't sound any different, but Rick's voice was softer than normal, more burp than belch.

"Clarify. It's not because you aren't a warrior. My planet would be dangerous for a warrior with tentacles." Any alien would be in danger, but Max had never gotten the computer to spit out a name for species outside one's own, so he had no way to say "alien" in alien-speak.

Rick did the half turn thing that meant he needed to study Max through a different set of eyes. Maybe different eyes tracked different wave lengths. Maybe they connected to different parts of the brain and Rick was trying to find some half-baked logic in Max's words.

Max caught Rick's tentacle in both his hands. "Query. Do you remember our discussion about why other species avoid the people?" Max asked, using Rick's name for his own species.

"Yes. They disapprove of the growing of offspring inside the body. They find us unsanitary. They are more group oriented and find our individual orientation unsettling. They question the cognitive complexity of offspring who are formed cognitively mature. They disapprove of volume and range of tones used for communication. They disgust at the people's lack of symmetry in form of body." Rick listed all the reasons as casually as someone might list ingredients in a pie.

Ironically, humans wouldn't have a problem with most of that. The belch-talking would be a huge hit on certain college campuses, although Rick did have a point about the lack of symmetry. That and the lack of a neck had made Max uncomfortable when he'd first taken the job. Now he liked Rick's appearance. The pale green of his skin contrasted the red-orange of the tips and undersides of his tentacles And his eyes were freaky, but that lack of symmetry moved them away from spider-like creepy to an oddly constructed stuffed-toy aesthetic.

But none of that would prevent humans from hating Rick. "My people don't need reasons to avoid others. They make reasons up."

"Correction. Max does not. Max is of his people. Logic is missing from the statement."

Max sighed. "I have hated illogically," he said, and when he thought about his own ridiculous hatred of all things touching on jock popularity, he knew he was right. He'd been uncomfortable with Pete even being on the football team because Max had looked down on the whole Neanderthal clique. He headed back to the bed and collapsed. "Some humans might accept you, but you will never be safe on Earth because some warriors will stop at nothing to kill you. They will be afraid. You will challenge their beliefs, but that has nothing to do with you. Those people would hate anyone who came to the planet for the same reason."

"Query. The safety of you." Rick moved close again.

That was the crux of the matter. Max sighed. "I don't know."

Rick's tentacles jerked and then curled into tight balls. "I change ship course." Rick twitched several times before he uncurled his tentacles enough to let go of the edge of the bed he had grabbed. And then, with most of his tentacles still tightly balled, he headed out.

"Wait." Max followed.

"No wait. No go Earth. No danger for Max." Rick was making pretty good time down the corridor, and Max ran after him.

"Wait a second. Just listen."

Rick reached the lift. "No listen. Max avoids pleasure to remain autonomous. Acceptable. Guards offspring. Acceptable. Puts himself at risk. Not acceptable."

"What?"

The lift opened, and Rick got in. The doors damn near closed before Max could get in with him. "Query. Clarify *avoids pleasure*." The lift jerked downward with far more speed than Max was used to.

"You produced seed when I activated your reproductive system."

Max blushed. "Yeah, I remember." Tentacle porn did live up to its name. It was the only kind of porn that did.

"You said to avoid sex because of emotions involved."

"I did not," Max protested.

A recording of Max's voice came through the computer. "However, sometimes sex involves how bodies fit together and the emotions that people feel for one another. That sex becomes complicated, and turning on the reproductive system too quickly can be a problem."

Max cringed. Okay, he had said that. The lift opened and Rick moved damn fast for a one-legged tentacle monster that imitated a snail's propulsion system. "I said the sex was complicated, not that I was avoiding it."

Rick didn't answer. He headed straight for the control room, and even when Max caught a couple of tentacles, Rick didn't stop. He dragged Max along for the ride.

"Will you talk to me?"

"Unacceptable risk. I will not allow Max to return to planet of danger." Rick touched the computer screen and a complex set of symbols projected out in three dimensions.

"We need to talk about this. You don't get to make decisions for me."

"You cannot reprogram ship for navigation, so I can make decision," Rick said.

Max ducked under a cluster of tentacles so he stood in the middle of the hologram. The light made him squint, but at least Rick stopped working the controls. "My people need to know the truth. My parents are back there. My brother is back there. I need to tell Earth that they were caught on the edge of a spaceship chase, not ground zero for an invasion."

"Illogical. Query. Logic of organized units to invade small, undeveloped planet in isolated territory."

Max sighed. "Because people fear. I have to tell them they can stop being afraid."

"They inspire fear. They have danger." Rick's whale song was loud enough to make Max's bones ache, and his tentacles were still curled. "Unacceptable."

"I have an obligation to my people."

Rick gave a huge belch before he backed away. "Reprogram navigation. I not stop. You fill obligation without me to navigate."

Max frowned. "You know I can't."

"I stop ship. You can restart when you learn navigation to navigate." A few of Rick's tentacles loosened, although he still was curled up enough to make his distress pretty damn clear.

"Rick," Max said softly.

"No! No move ship. You move ship." As if to make a point, Rick backed farther from the controls.

Max dropped onto the couch. Rick might have been impressed by Max's background as a military man, but not enough to listen. And Rick was right about one thing: Max couldn't fly the ship. He put his hands to his face. After a few minutes, Rick touched him. A tentacle slid over Max's shoulder and then encircled his upper arm. Max looked up.

"Sorries. Many sorries. No danger to Max." Rick crept closer.

Max sighed. "I understand the danger."

"You warrior. Warriors never protect enough self."

"You're wrong about that," Max said. Service members were people, and in the end, most did put insane amounts of energy into saving themselves. Those who earned military honors garnered so much respect because self-sacrifice was the exception—not the rule.

"Not returning to Earth Max." Rick stretched his tentacles out stiffly.

"I don't think I even want to go back, not now," Max said. "But I still have to tell Earth the truth. They need to know they're safe. My parents need to know I'm alive." Max definitely planned to skip the part where they were sort of grandparents.

"Query. Explain." Rick stopped after those two words.

Max wasn't sure where to begin. "I miss parts of Earth. You would like music. I think. You would like our oceans. I like to think you and my parents would get along." Max frowned. That might be pushing it. His parents were supportive, but his father got a sour expression any time Max brought up being gay. Gay and fathering tentacle babies would probably push their tolerance too far.

"Query. Max prefers to return."

"No." The Air Force would court martial him if they found out he was choosing Rick over the service, but Max didn't care. He might if the Office of Special Investigations had a branch in space, but it was human ignorance for the win on that front. If they wanted to charge him with being a deserter, they would have to build the space ship that could find him first. And really, considering how he had left Earth, they would have listed him as Missing in Action.

Rick's tentacles uncurled.

"I like the ship and you and the offspring. I like protecting the ship, and I want to know how those invaders managed to get onboard without any alarms going off, and we are going to fix that problem," Max said. Rick curled a few tentacles around Max's arm. "But I want to get close enough to Earth to send them a message."

More tentacles curled around Max's leg.

"And I am not trying to avoid sex. I didn't want to have sex when I liked you. I was afraid you only wanted me for the offspring and I wanted to avoid having my feelings shredded." Max was fairly sure the translator would choke on that bit of emotional bloodletting.

Rick pressed forward, claiming a space between Max's knees. "You fear tangling tentacles. You fear damage."

Max huffed. Maybe the translator worked better than he'd thought.

"You are warrior," Rick said, and Max got the feeling that Rick used that word to mean something between a comic book hero and a super soldier. Max wasn't either.

"I can still hurt. Hell, you're a lot stronger than I am," Max said. Some days Max felt like a windshield with a tiny spider web crack in the corner. One bit of pressure on the wrong point and he would shatter.

"Max stronger. Rick better with computers," Rick said.

Max laughed. "That you are." His whole body felt stiff and sore. Giving up Earth had sapped him of all his strength. His stomach bruising felt worse than ever and his head was throbbing in time with his heartbeat. "I think I should go lie down," he said. "Maybe in that nice new bed of mine."

Max stood, and Rick held onto his leg for a few extra seconds. Feeling about a thousand years old, Max moved toward his new quarters. Later he would have to get the one pair of spare pants that constituted his worldly possessions, but for now, all he wanted was sleep.

Chapter Twenty-Two

Max woke to find a heavy weight on his left side. He cracked his eyes open to find Rick taking up at least two thirds of the mattress. All those bright, black inquisitive eyes were closed and most of his tentacles were curled up under him, which gave him a squat look that hit Max's cute button. Something was different. When Max touched his stomach, most of the bruising was gone. Rick had been using his healing trick again; he had missed his calling as a professional mother hen.

Two of Rick's smaller eyes opened and then all the others followed.

"Good morning," Max said.

"Healthy awakenings," Rick returned.

"Query. Did you happen to fix any swelling and bruising while I was asleep?"

"Beds contain medical facilities equivalent to the lower lab." Rick touched the overhead controls, and alien script filled the screen. "Technology remove toxins and reduced blood pooling at site of injury."

That sounded like a cure for bruising. Technology for the win.

"The window of Max's eye has returned to normal," Rick said.

"Correction. The pupil of my eye is not dilated." It had never occurred to Max that Rick could read his emotional state as easily as Max could track those curling tentacles. Max had never yelled or panicked, yet Rick had known. He had taken one look at the "window" of Max's eye and known how much Max feared going home. "I still need to send them a message. I don't want them afraid."

Rick was silent for a time. "I can move ship close enough to transmit sound. Query. Will they listen?"

"I think they have every bit of technology they own pointed at the skies to listen. But even if they aren't listening, I have to try."

"Acceptable," Rick agreed. "I do not hope for fear in humans. I like humans."

"Unfortunately, humans would probably be afraid of you. You have too many limbs." Max had pretty well let the cat out of the bag, so he didn't feel any need to hide the worst of humanity.

"To evaluate on appearance is common."

Max huffed. He knew Rick was trying to make him feel better, but Max was more than a little embarrassed to have come from a planet where someone as kind as Rick would be dismissed as a monster.

"Others evaluate the people as undesirable for lack of symmetry. Humans are much symmetry more." Rick ran a tentacle over Max's forehead and then down his nose.

"My symmetry is superficial. Inside, I am not symmetrical," Max pointed out.

"This I know. This others know. But humans' exterior appearance symmetrical. Others find symmetry pleasing."

"And how do you find symmetry?" Max asked. "That was a query."

Rick pulled more tentacles out from under his body and draped several over Max's stomach. "Symmetry is predictable. It lacks surprise or element to inspire exploration."

Max supplied the word Rick struggled to express. "Boring. You find symmetry boring." That did make some sense. Every time Rick turned his head, a whole new pattern of eyes and colors appeared. From a distance, he appeared light green, but up close, Rick's skin had streaks of greens and beiges. And then the undersides and ends of the tentacles were vivid reds and oranges. If someone took a hundred pictures of Rick, no two would look the same. There was a lot to explore.

"Max is not boring," Rick said. He wrapped his tentacles around Max's middle and squeezed.

"I am symmetrical, at least externally."

"But internally asymmetrical. Rick rested a tentacle on his lower stomach. "Internally, Max is random and unpredictable."

Max narrowed his eyes. "Are you saying you find my intestines attractive?" Of all the pickup lines. Max had gotten in his life, and he had gotten a lot, that was the oddest.

"Yes."

"You're the weird one."

Rick shimmied. "Max is unpredictable with actions. He is warrior who will surrogate. He is father who will claim genetic otherness as his own." Rick stretched, and his tentacle brushed over Max's half hard cock. Immediately, Rick froze, his tentacle still pressing Max's genitals, and alien pants were not nearly thick enough to hide what was going on. "Query. Would you tangle tentacles?"

Max was bordering on desperate to have sex, and his cock was getting harder by the second. However, he knew better than to crap where he ate. At least he did now. As a teen and even a young man in his early twenties, he had slept with too many people he worked with or had class with. It had made for some awkward morning-afters. "Tangling tentacles can make it difficult for me to leave. You said your people never stay, that you swim away."

"Children must leave a parent. To stay with a parent is to remain in stagnant water."

"Well, humans like water which does not move," Max said. "If we tangle tentacles, I'll want the waters to not move, so it's best if we don't get tangled." Max rolled away from Rick.

Most of Rick's tentacles slid away as Max sat up on the edge of the bed, but Rick curled one tentacle around Max's wrist. "Children swim away from parents. Young ones swim away from the city of birth. The people explore."

Max sighed and pushed Rick's last tentacle off. "Yeah. I get it. And that's why we shouldn't tangle tentacles."

"You do not understand." Rick caught Max's wrist again before Max could flee this awkward conversation. "Adults do not flee from every attachment. When the people have explored enough, as elders we seek to bond in a stagnant pairing."

Max scooted around so he could look at Rick. "Are you saying you are old enough to pair bond?" This conversation was spinning out of control even faster than yesterday's.

"I am not," Rick said, and Max's chest tightened. He needed to stop emotionally relying on Rick. "But I am willing to remain in stagnant waters, which are interesting."

That sounded like an alien version of a pity fuck, or maybe a pity relationship. Max wasn't exactly following the conversation well enough to tell, but pity was involved, and Max didn't do pity. "I don't want to be the stagnant waters you endure.

"Query. Clarification. To endure is negative."

"Yes," Max blurted. "And I don't want you to accept a negative because you think..." Max struggled for the words.

"I endure nothing." Rick pulled Max back onto the bed. "Stagnant water is pleasant to one who has traveled fast streams."

Max closed his eyes. This was painful because it came so close to what Max wanted, and yet it was a world apart from real commitment or desire.

"I sought offspring because I hoped for slower waters. I could not hope to find a pair bond. Query. Would you pair bond?"

Max's brain had a full meltdown. "What?"

"To pair bond is to share stagnant waters and enjoy the condition of boring with an individual you find pleasing enough to seek repetitious experiences."

Max blinked and tried to restart his brain. "That is the strangest definition of marriage I have ever heard," he said in a weak voice. He cleared his throat. "Query. Are you asking me to marry you? Oh, wait. Better question. Query. How long does pair bonding last?"

"Many years. Until one seeks faster water."

"Oh. So it's a marriage with a built-in divorce. Great." Max needed to avoid emotional entanglements.

Rick pushed himself to the edge of the bed and let half his tentacles spill over the edge. "Query. Markers for unhappiness."

"Most humans would hope their marriage would last forever." Max rubbed his face. "Divorce is when a pair bonding ends with the partners wanting to leave the bond before death. The pair goes to elders to request resources can be fairly divided so each can swim in other waters." That was a big of a simplification since plenty of married people Max knew swam in plenty of other, faster waters without getting a divorce first, but hopefully Rick would see the problem. Max was built for the whole death-do-part routine. He'd grown up in a small town where people still whispered words like divorce and infidelity in mock horror as they gossiped.

"To involve elders would be seen as a lack of skill in ending a pair bond successfully."

"I can't argue with that." Max added a weak chuckle. "But we need to avoid tangling tentacles because humans want forever. Ending a pair bond usually includes screaming and blame and much damage."

"Clarify. Emotional damage or physical damage?"

"Both," Max said. "Well, most of the damage is emotional, but it is not unusual for the violence to turn physical." Max edited out the part where people even killed over pair bonding from time to time. He had already made humans sound like psychopaths, but he didn't want to make it worse.

"Max is never stagnant-bad even if we are stagnant-unchanging," Rick said.

Max ran his fingers over one of Rick's larger tentacles. "That is the nicest thing anyone has said to me in a long time."

"Clarify. Long time."

"Years," Max said. "You are kinder than anyone I've known for years."

Rick shimmied. "I understand your warning of danger inherent within human pair bonds. I still wish to pair bond."

"I don't know that it is safe for us to pair bond." That was not technically true since Max knew full well it was unsafe. He had too many tangled emotions. Maybe that was the isolation or the children. Or maybe his feelings for Rick, but if this relationship went sideways, Max would be screwed in the unfun way.

Instead of withdrawing, Rick curled more tentacles around Max. "I am smart. I am knowing that humans have dangerous instincts. I am knowing Max is dangerous. I still want pair bond."

Max sucked in a fast breath. "I would never hurt you. I don't care how bad our relationship ended. I don't care if you dropped me on a planet on the far side of the universe. I would not hurt you." Max's guts roiled.

"Okay."

Max frowned because he had no idea what that meant. "I wouldn't," he said.

"I believe." The wrinkles around Rick's eyes deepened.

"I'm not afraid for you. I fear I will hurt if you choose to swim away. Me."

Rick didn't answer for a long time. They sat on the edge of the bed and Max felt like they were teetering on some tipping point. He had already agreed to stay on the ship, so he wasn't sure why Rick was pushing for sex. "I like Max's stagnant water," Rick said so slowly that the translation computer had to pause between words. "I like Max's stories. I like Max keeping offspring safe. I like Max keeping me safe. I like Max happy and making strange mouth noises."

"Clarify. Laughing. Those mouth noises are laughing," Max said.

Again, Rick was silent for a significant amount of time before he responded. "I like Max laughing."

Max's defenses were crumbling faster than he could shore them up. He *wanted* a connection. That made it hard to stick to his stoic celibacy. He shrugged. "That's not the worst reason to pair bond."

"Query. Max pair bond Rick."

Max knew he should say no. He should retain some semblance of independence. He just didn't want to. He was tired of being alone, and that feeling was much older than getting lost in space. He whispered his answer. "Yes."

Rick's tentacles quivered before curling around Max's torso.

Almost immediately, tentacles crept up and under Max's shirt. It wasn't an unusual response to accepting a proposal, but Max didn't know what to do with his hands. He stroked a tentacle, but he had no idea what passed for an erogenous zone on an alien. "I don't know what to do," Max admitted. He hadn't said that since he was twelve years old and had discovered porn. Porn had given him a lot of bad advice, but at least he was doing something, even if it was the completely wrong something for the situation.

"Tangle tentacles." Rick curled a tentacle around Max's wrist. All of those mini tentacles along the underside tangled around Max's fingers. Max stretched his fingers and then closed his fist. Rick shivered.

"If that's what does it for you, I can tangle some tentacles." Max shifted to the right so that he could lean back and pull his legs up. He caught one of Rick's tentacles between his two legs and then locked his ankles together in a wrestling move. Rick gave a full body shiver.

Then Rick was pulling at the shirt so hard that Max feared having underarm bruises. "Hey, don't tear it. It's the only one I have."

"We fabricate more. Many more." Rick blurted the words out almost too fast for the translator.

"Yes, but you're going to bruise me."

Rick stopped pulling the fabric. Buttons weren't his thing, so Max shook his hand free of the tentacles that held him. In a second, he had unfastened several buttons. Rick got the message because several tentacles detoured from pulling duty and started unbuttoning. He shoved the shirt off Max's shoulders, but it got caught right around Max's elbows. "I can take it off," Max offered.

Rick shifted to Max's pants without giving him time to wiggle free of his shirt. Max unbuttoned his pants before Rick could do any damage. It had taken him forever to get the computer to fabricate a decent crotch and he didn't want to lose a pair of pants. As soon as Max got the zipper down, tentacles pushed his hand out of the way.

Tiny finger tentacles grabbed his cock, and Max arched his back, but Rick tightened his tentacles around Max's arms, thwarting any attempt to flail. And Max did attempt. Strenuously. His cock turned painfully hard before Rick had even started pushing the pants down around Max's thighs.

"Oh shit."

"Query. Am I being shitty?" Rick asked, all his tentacles freezing in place.

"No!" Max screamed the word. "You're awesome. Shit is an expression of strong emotion. In this case, good emotion." Very good. Max might regret this later when he got his heart broken, but right now his body enthusiastically approved.

"I do not approve."

"Yeah, well don't stop," Max said. Slowly the tentacles started moving again, undulating against Max's bare flesh. One rested right over Max's left nipple, then suction pulled on his skin. Rick experimented, sucking first hard and then soft. Max threw his head back and panted as his awareness narrowed to the small piece of flesh where Rick experimented with different sensations. Finger tentacles slid over his skin and then a dozen suckers all went to work. Max groaned as tentacles writhed and contorted, knotted with each other and then darted around Max's arms and hands, his legs and neck, and finally his cock.

The sucking sensation was everywhere, some soft enough to tickle and others so strong that Max squirmed under the onslaught. He grabbed a handful of tentacles, holding tightly. Rick shuddered and then curled his tentacles around Max's fingers and wrist. When Rick pulled his right hand up, the shirt still caught around his biceps tightened and then he dragged Max up the bed. Rick shifted so his huge head rested over Max's thighs, the heavy weight pinning Max to the bed.

Then tentacles encircled his ankles. Max used his limited mobility to hook his ankle around one of them and pull on it. Rick's shiver was smaller, but with his weight on Max, Max felt it and a tremor went up his own back. That made Rick shiver again. Rick had explored much of Max's body, those suckers teasing him everywhere, but now they returned to Max's nipples. One tentacle covered both nipples and sucked hard. Max bucked. He dug his heels into the bed and lifted Rick into the air, but Rick was heavy, and Max collapsed back onto the bed. However, in the short time he'd had his ass up, tentacles had darted under him.

Rick wrapped a thick tentacle around the small of Max's back. It left Max's ass suspended a few inches above the bed, and this was the most vulnerable, hottest sex position Max had ever experienced. Max shook his right hand free of the tentacles around it before he grabbed a thicker one the way he would grab a rope during PT. He circled the tentacle until it was wrapped around his forearm and then he grasped it. Smaller tentacles twined around their joined arms.

A tentacle slid across Max's inner thigh before brushing Max's cock. Max gasped. It felt slick and the small finger tentacles teased the sensitive skin.

"Humans and the people much compatible," Rick said in a low and rumbly voice.

Max agreed, but he didn't have the brain cells to form words. Gentle suction teased Max's cock and the tiny fingers tormented him, exploring the head of his cock. Max tried to thrust up, but Rick had captured both of his legs and the tentacle at the small of his back had curled around his hips so he was firmly held. Max suspected Rick was using his strong leg tentacle to bind him, but the one around Max's throat made it impossible for him to look down to check.

"Please." A needy moan escaped, and for a half second, Max tried to maintain some sort of dignity. But then Rick tightened his hold on Max's cock while dragging a tentacle across his hole. Max threw all restraint out and thrashed. "Fuck. Yes. More." His one word demands ended when Rick thrust deep into him.

Pleasure crashed through him. Max's cock was so hard that it hurt, and he would have come if not for the tentacles wrapped tightly around the base. Max didn't want to be an inconsiderate lover, lying back while the other guy did all the work, but his limbs were tangled in tentacles. He could only writhe in need. A tentacles passed over his lips, and Max sucked at the pale skin. At first he kept his explorations tentative and gentle, but when Rick shivered, Max sucked harder.

The tentacle in his ass pushed in. Rick's limbs were cool, which contrasted with his hot body pressing down against Max's belly and thighs. The tentacle forced Max's body to stretch until muscle strained and stung.

"Wait!" Max cried. Everything froze. Rick's tentacles still held him in an iron grip, but nothing sucked or teased or pushed. "Query. You aren't putting more offspring in me, are you?" Max asked. The blind lust faded. Fuck, did women have to worry about this every damn time? How the hell did they ever get their rocks off?

"No. I would not use Max as surrogate without conversation."

"Good. You ask before you put babies up there, and you ask when I'm not so hard that I could die if you don't shove more tentacle in me.

I would pretty much agree to anything at this point, including carrying a whole litter of offspring, so get your tentacles moving."

Unfortunately, Rick didn't budge. "Clarify. More offspring in future?"

"Many more, but right now, move your damn tentacles."

Rick shimmied and then shoved in so hard that Max screamed. The tentacle around Max's cock sucked and teased in time with the one in his ass. Every time the tentacle in his ass pulsed or bulged or thrust, the one around his cock would suck harder. Caught between the two sensations, Max cried out in pleasure.

The tip of Rick's tentacle probed the corner of Max's mouth, and Max turned his head toward it. He sucked at it and ran his tongue along the red underside where Rick had his tiny finger tentacles. The tentacle explored Max's mouth for a few seconds before Rick thrust it farther in and twined it around Max's tongue. Max pushed and sucked in a battle for his mouth that mimicked the one going on in his ass, but he was happily losing on both fronts.

Rick pulled his legs farther into the air and the tentacle in Max's ass felt twice as large. He screamed around the one in his mouth, and then he was coming. The pain made the world white out, but then Rick loosened his grip on Max's cock, and Max had the most glorious orgasm of his life. His muscles jerked and he fought Rick's hold. The tentacle around his leg slipped free, and Max dug the heel into the bed as his whole body turned into one over-stimulated nerve.

The hot, blind hunger faded, and Rick lowered him to the bed while Max panted. Rick pulled his tentacles out from under Max, but he left the one in Max's ass in place. Max felt like he was skewered, and he liked that far more than he would have expected. When he'd left toys in, they'd been uncomfortable, but Rick's tentacle fit. Max pushing himself farther up the bed, and the way the tentacle was dragged along with him was completely hot

"Did you come?" Max asked before adding a belated, "Query."

"Clarify come."

Max didn't have the brain cells for this. "Query. Did you reach maximum pleasure?"

"I am still feeling pleasure," Rick said, and the tentacle in Max's ass shivered.

"You are fond of my intestines, aren't you?" Max asked. He hadn't properly marked that as a question, so he didn't expect an answer. He got one anyway.

Rick shifted so his head rested on Max's chest, although his tentacle was just as deeply buried inside Max. "I am fond of your intestines. They are beautifully asymmetrical."

Max laughed and held his hand out, fingers spread, and Rick coiled his smallest tentacle around his fingers. Despite all their differences, they were pretty damn compatible.

Chapter Twenty-Three

Max studied the pattern of hickeys that crisscrossed his chest. It looked as if he'd been attacked by a swarm of tiny mouths, each one leaving a dime-sized red mark. Max ran his thumb over one that crossed onto his areola. The skin was sensitive and hot.

Rick walked up behind Max and touched Max's bare side. "Query. Have I damaged you?"

"No. Human lovers often leave marks like this. We call them hickeys."

"Observation. We have much different internal structures. You are rare boned-tentacle species. Of contrast, we are sexually compatible."

"Yes, we are," Max said with a smile. He grabbed his shirt from the floor. "I enjoyed that a lot."

Rick gave a little full-body shimmy. Rick followed Max and this time he wrapped several tentacles around Max's left arm. "Query. Why do you fear to be hurt?"

That pretty much killed the afterglow. Max let his right hand fall to his side. He considered running for the hills, only the ship didn't have hills. Worse, Rick would never understand it if Max fled. He would assume he had done something wrong. Finding out that Max was a warrior had clearly thrown Rick, and there was a certain insecurity there. Max didn't want to poke any emotional holes. "I think sometimes relationships are more complicated than people can handle," Max said. "And I think this relationship is complicated because we don't always understand each other."

"Clarify. Complicated."

Max huffed. He knew he had programmed that word, but he'd defined the way it applied to a control center having too many buttons or a diagram too many lines. But really, it wasn't that much different with relationships. They had too many differences between them, and wanting this to last forever didn't change any of the obstacles they would have to overcome. Right now, Rick might be impressed with himself for getting a warrior into his bed, but sooner or later he would want to tangle tentacles with someone who had tentacles. Max spread the fingers of his left hand and the tips of Rick's tentacles wound between them. "Clarify," Max said, "complicated is having too many working pieces to watch all of them at once."

"I have many eyes. I can watch many pieces."

Max let out a bark of laughter. "You do have many asymmetrical eyes."

"Thank you."

The smile faded from Max's face. "I don't know if even you have enough eyes to watch all the potential problems with the relationship."

Rick was silent for a long time. He stood with his bulbous head resting against Max's shoulder and little tentacle fingers stroking Max's left arm. "I understand," he said eventually. "Relationship between species requires ignoring of unpleasant attributes."

"Query. Like my symmetrical eyes?" Max asked.

"I overlook the flaw because you cannot prevent unfortunate symmetry. I remember much your intestines," Rick said in a serious tone.

Max had nothing to say to that. He'd had lovers with fetishes in the past, but never had someone cared about intestinal tracts. Sure, as a gay man he'd played with his butt, but he saw his intestines more as a shortcut to the prostate than an attractive feature in and of itself.

"Query. Is there some trait of me that you cannot overlook?" Rick asked. He withdrew some of his tentacles.

"No!" Max tightened his fingers around Rick's tentacles. "Right now, you seem like the perfect lover. And that's what scares me. Because when we figure out why this isn't going to work, it will hurt to lose you." A surge of emotion slammed into Max.

"You are warrior." Rick pulled onto the bed.

"Query. Why say that now?"

Rick wound a few more tentacles around Max's arm. "Warrior seeks to identify dangers. It is the nature of warrior. You seek trouble and danger in relationship. You can look and look and look and look and look and when you see I will not leave, then you can stop feeling warrior fear."

"I..." Max stopped. His mother used to tell him that he borrowed trouble from the future, that he was unwilling to even wait for disasters to come before he anticipated them. And he had taken a lot of emotional hits in the last year or so. Too many. A human psychiatrist would probably tell him that he needed time to recover before he made big decisions, like deciding a relationship was doomed because one half of the couple lacked bones in their tentacles.

"Query. You enjoy entangling tentacles."

If Max didn't know better, he would say Rick was manipulating him by changing the subject. "You are a sex God. That was the best orgasm of my life, and I enjoyed the sex so much that I have no right to be negative." Hopefully Rick understood that was an apology.

"Feelings exist. The others have feelings about asymmetry. Illogical feelings. Query. Would you dislike me if I had an even number of tentacles?"

"Of course not." Max hadn't ever counted the tentacles.

"Logical." Rick gave a little bounce.

Max shook his head. Aliens. So weird. "I do have one question about staying, though."

Rick stilled. "Query. You doubt staying?"

"No. No I will stay. But I have one query. Query. Will you give me the information and authority to make sure that no one ever gets on the ship again?"

"Query. Clarify to circumscribe request." Rick tilted his head to the side.

"Clarify language. Explain the parameters of the request," Max corrected the translation. "Clarify request. I need access to any security you have on the ship because it is not enough. Someone got on the ship and I didn't hear a single alarm."

"Alarm interrupts difficult mathematical calculations."

For a second, Max lost the ability to form words. After several false starts, he demanded, "Are you saying you turned the alarms off?"

"Alarms are distracting." Rick leaned away.

Max shivered at the idea of floating through space with absolutely no warning system. "Okay. That won't happen again. We can reroute the alarms so only I hear it, but if someone docks with this ship, I need to know."

"Acceptable. I underestimated the ability of others to detect my movements."

"Yes. You did. In fact... query. Do we have some sensors that would tell us if another ship was near?"

"Query. Clarify near."

Max's military training kicked in and he started wondering about the operational specs of the weapons enemies might use. He had learned to fight in airspace defined by gravity and the physics of propulsion systems in Earth atmosphere. The underlying understanding of strategy would be similar, but all the specifics would be different in space. "I don't know how near. I need to study warrior information in the ship's computer. I need to know what species are out there and which ones are dangerous. I need to know what weapons are most common and which ones will give me horrible burns in close proximity." Max's arms tingled. "I need to know the vulnerabilities of various spacecraft and of different species. To protect my family, I need information, and I need you to let me make changes required to protect this family." Max braced himself for any number of counter arguments. After all, humans didn't even possess space technology, so giving Max that sort of information could be seen as irresponsible.

Instead, Rick simply said, "Acceptable." He walked out.

Max dashed after him. "Query. Clarify. Acceptable. What part are you accepting?"

"All. I am not warrior. You know warrior needs more than I. I will open all information and resources so you may be warrior."

"No questions?"

"You may ask questions," Rick said as they got into the lift. "But I have no warrior skill. You should not trust my words on warrior craft. I am good with computer command systems."

"Yeah, I figured out that first part," Max said. He still couldn't believe Rick had turned off the damn alarm. Rick had no tactical sense, none at all. The lift doors opened, and Max followed Rick as they headed toward the control room.

"Computers in upper ship give access unallowed to..." The computer lost the last word, but it confirmed Max's assumption that the area below the control room was for the hired help or maybe paying passengers. "Computer in the room of Max or rooms of study on levels will give full warrior information."

They passed through the control room and headed toward the pool room. "Why is the pool in the area with less access?" Max asked.

"Offspring are small. They cannot learn skill for compensation now. They will want to swim in faster waters faster than they should."

"Awwww. You're an overprotective father." Max shoulder-bumped Rick.

Rick curled his tentacles around Max's arm. "You are father even more overprotect. Earth fathers are weird."

"You've said that before."

"Is worth saying multiple times," Rick said. He pulled Max close enough that Max's legs brushed his tentacles with each step. When they walked into the pool room, Kohei and Xander were swimming, but James was nowhere to be seen. The boy was probably off exploring or getting himself in trouble. Or both. He was going to give Max gray hair before he was grown.

"Rick father! Max father!" Xander called. He zipped to the edge of the pool. "Come swim with us."

"Come swim," Kohei echoed.

"What do you say, Rick. Query. Would you like to swim?" Max asked.

"Yes." Rick blasted the air with whale song, and James's head appeared out from behind a large pipe.

"Reduce the volume." Max stripped off his shirt. Maybe the fabricators in the upper level would be able to turn out a shirt that fit. Max could always ask James to help. He was good with computers, although making shirts wouldn't keep his interest for long.

"Many sorries for soft, symmetrical human ears," Rick said as he waded into the pool and reached for Xander.

"Asshole," Max grumbled.

"Asshole!" Kohei repeated in a far louder voice.

"Don't say that." Max pulled his pants off so he could swim in his underwear. Rick threw Xander into the air. When Xander splashed down, he made a squealing noise and flailed his tentacles.

Kohei swam to the edge of the pool. "Max father said it."

"Max father says things you shouldn't." Max stopped ankle deep in the pool. "Shit. I've turned into my father." While Max was distracted with the horror of that, Rick swam up and caught his ankle. In a heartbeat, Rick pulled Max's leg out from under him. Max fell backward and had a half second to imagine bashing his head in on the edge of the pool. Then Rick wrapped him up in tentacles so Max splashed safely down in the shallows.

"You asshole!" Max shouted. He splashed Rick with both hands, but Rick just blew bubbles and pulled him deeper into the water.

"Save Max father," James cried, and then he flung himself into the pool and started splashing madly. The boy had the worst aim, because most of the water went straight up into the air and landed on him. However, Kohei joined the fight, and he could kick up huge amounts of water. Max turned his head to the side to protect himself from the deluge.

After releasing Max, Rick jetted toward Kohei. Abandoning his attack, Kohei fled toward the water filtration island. Rick chased. Laughing, Max watched them dart around. James got into the middle of it, but Max couldn't tell whose side he was on. He seemed to like random splashing.

"Query. Max father leave for home soon?" Xander asked as he climbed Max's arm to settle in on his shoulder.

"I'm not leaving at all," Max said. "This is home."

For a moment Xander didn't stir a tentacle, but then he flung himself down into the water and blasted out a miniature version of his father's whale song. The translator missed most of the message, but it did spit out "Max" "stay" and "father."

James and Kohei stopped. After a few seconds of listening to their little brother, both swam toward Max. But instead of catching him up in a bear hug, all three offspring began singing and splashing Max violently enough that he could only shield himself as he laughed so hard that he had trouble even catching his breath, much less retaliating.

"I protect Max!" Rick announced, and then he slapped up a tidal wave that drenched everyone, including Max.

"Watch the friendly fire!" Max yelled as he used one hand to shovel water in the general direction of the boys and Rick.

Max was outgunned in this fight, but somehow, he didn't mind. Maybe he hadn't chosen to get dragged into space, but if he ever found that alien ship that had invaded Earth's atmosphere, he might buy them a good bottle of whatever passed for beer in these part. Without them, Max never would have figured out where his real home was.

Epilogue

Max settled down in front of the camera and took a deep breath. Rick had offered to appear on camera as well, but as much as Max appreciated him and all his tentacley glory, he would not go over well with humans. So Max perched on the edge of the seat and tried to look calm and composed.

"This is Captain Maxwell Davis of the United States Air Force, 4th Fighter Squadron out of Hill. This message is for any authorities on Earth. Earth was not invaded. Earth is on the edge of populated space and aliens have no interest in the planet. The alien ships that violated Earth space almost a year ago were on an intergalactic car chase.

"Some sort of authority—either a civilian peacekeeping force or a military force, I'm unclear which—chased a ship of criminals called the Nish into the largely unpopulated corner of the universe where Earth sits. When my F-35 was damaged, aliens brought me into their ship to save me.

"However, they returned to their own space, either in pursuit of the Nish or because the pursuit had ended—I'm not sure which. I am doing well, but transportation back to Earth is exceptionally expensive. Earth is far from any trade paths, so it will take me years to earn enough money to purchase a ticket home.

"Since I cannot return to provide a report, I hope this message reaches the correct authorities. The universe is well-established with space-faring species. Most come from roughly Earth-sized planets, and most engage in regulated trade through neutral planets. The government authorities who took me from Earth released me at one of these trade ports, and the alien equivalent of a social worker taught me how to use their technology to secure employment.

"I work for a computer programmer, providing security for him, his three offspring, and his ship. Much of my information comes from this individual, who I refer to as 'Rick.' His name does not translate, and neither does the name of his species, which he simply refers to as *the people.*

"However, I can say that his species is unpopular because they are asymmetrical, and they find the more popular races boring because Rick's people dislike symmetry. So the universe judges on appearance. Humans are not unique in that. However, we are biologically rare. The vast majority of all these species have tentacles. I've worked with a computer translation program to differentiate *limb*, but I've have questionable results. The aliens perceive an arm as little more than a tentacle with a motion-limiting internal skeleton.

"I hope someone will contact my parents, Richard and Velma Davis, and my brother Peter Davis and tell them that I am safe and gainfully employed. Every day I improve the computer language interface and learn about the universe.

"Right now I can only say that the universe is interesting. They have criminals, so it's not a utopia out here. However, these people are technologically advanced and generally friendly, although some aliens are on the condescending side.

"The ship I am on is close enough to Earth that we are broadcasting this message toward the planet. I have asked Rick to repeat my message as long as we are in this sector of space, but we are heading toward populated areas, so I don't know how many repetitions Rick will broadcast.

"This is Captain Maxwell Davis signing off. Take care of each other, Earth."

Lyn Gala

Lyn Gala started writing in the back of her science notebook in third grade and hasn't stopped since. Westerns starring men with shady pasts gave way to science fiction with questionable protagonists, which eventually became any story with a morally ambiguous character. Even the purest heroes have pain and loss and darkness in their hearts, and that's where she likes to find her stories. Her characters seek to better themselves and find the happy (or happier) ending.

When she isn't writing, Lyn Gala teaches history in a small town in New Mexico. Her favorite spot to write is a flat rock under a wide tree on the edge of the open desert where her dog can terrorize local wildlife. Writing in a wide range of genres, she often gravitates back to adventure and BDSM, stories about men in search of true love and a way to bring some criminal to justice...unless *they* happen to be the criminals.

Don't miss out!

Visit the website below and you can sign up to receive emails whenever Lyn Gala publishes a new book. There's no charge and no obligation.

https://books2read.com/r/B-A-DWFG-NQIY

BOOKS 2 READ

Connecting independent readers to independent writers.

Did you love *Earth Fathers Are Weird*? Then you should read *Claimings, Tails, and Other Alien Artifacts* by Lyn Gala!

Liam loves his life as a linguist and trader on the Rownt homeworld, but he has ignored his heart and sexual needs for years. After escaping the horrors of war, he wants a boring life. He won't risk letting anyone come too close because he won't risk letting anyone see his deeply submissive nature. For him, submission comes with pain. Life burned that lesson into his soul from a young age. This fear keeps him from noticing that the Rownt trader Ondry cares for him. Ondry may not understand humans, but he recognizes a wounded soul, and his need to protect Liam is quickly outpacing his common sense. They may have laws, culture, and incompatible genitalia in their way, but Ondry knows that he can find a way to overcome all that if he can just overcome the ghosts of Liam's past. Only then can he take possession of a man he has grown to respect.

Also by Lyn Gala

Standalone
Bitter Blood
Blowback
Two Steps Back
Clockwork Pirate
Earth Fathers Are Weird

www.ingramcontent.com/pod-product-compliance
Ingram Content Group UK Ltd.
Pitfield, Milton Keynes, MK11 3LW, UK
UKHW010719290525
6137UKWH00028B/115

9 781393 605461